A Station Named Liligumma
&
Other Rail Stories

Krupa Sagar Sahoo

Translated by
Malabika Patel

Leadstart
INKSTATE

ISBN 978-93-90266-82-1
Copyright © Krupa Sagar Sahoo, 2020

First published in India 2021 by Leadstart Inkstate
A Division of One Point Six Technologies Pvt Ltd

Sales Office:
Unit No.25/26, Building No.A/1,
Near Wadala RTO,
Wadala (East), Mumbai – 400037 India
Phone: +91 969933000
Email: info@leadstartcorp.com
www.leadstartcorp.com

Disclaimer: The views expressed in this book are those of the Author and do not pertain to be held by the Publisher.

Editor: Ateendriya Dasgupta
Cover: Ami Parekh
Illustrator: Debendranath Laha
Layouts: Kshitij Dhawale

To Shri A. Ramji, ex-General Manager S.E. Railway—a friend, philosopher and guide for the junior officers.

About the Author

Krupa Sagar Sahoo is a Senior Ex-Railway Officer (Retd. IRTS Officer), who served the Indian Railways for thirty-four years from 1978 to 2012. During this tenure he was posted in various zones of Indian Railways and had the good fortune to draw inspiration from his experiences with people at work and life in general. More than fifty of his short stories have Indian Railways as the theme. His style of subtle humour has earned him a niche in Odia literature. Nature in all its manifestations, animals, birds, and the common man are also some of the recurring themes in his writings. Today, he is a leading name in Odia literature, with thirteen short story collections and six novels to his credit. Many of his stories have been translated into English and other major Indian languages and have been appreciated by his readers.

Shri Sahoo was a recipient of Odisha Sahitya Academy Award 2009 for his original novel ***Shesha Sarat***, which has been translated to English under the title ***Chilika: A Love Story.***

Address of Author:
Krupa Sagar Sahoo
Plot No 255, District Centre,
Chandrasekharpur, Bhubaneswar
Odisha - 751016

Contact No: 09437170033
Mail id: krupasagarsahoo1952@gmail.com
Website: www.krupasagarsahoo.com

Contents

Other Rail Stories

Translator's Note

In Indian literature, stories with the railways serving as a backdrop are not uncommon. The *Penguin Book of Indian Railway Stories*, edited by the indubitable Ruskin Bond, contains masterpieces from the master storytellers, the likes of which include Khushwant Singh, Jim Corbett, Rudyard Kipling, and Manoj Das. Their famous short stories revolving around the Indian Railways were mostly written before or just after Independence. In the words of Mark Twain, the stories showed the fascination of the writers with the "perennially ravishing show of Indian railway stations".

Odia short story writer Shri Krupa Sagar Sahoo's fascination with Indian Railways, however, is of a different genre. His narrative revolves around the people who serve the Indian Railways. His anthology of railway stories was first published in an Odia short story collection, *Rail Galpa* (2011), which was followed by an English translation of some of the stories under the title *Rail Romance* (2018). The stories were contemporary; they were placed during the last two decades of twentieth century and written from an insider's perspective. There is a reason that Shri Sahoo wrote extensively on the railway folks. As an Indian Railways Traffic Service officer, he served for thirty-four years (1978–2012) in the states of Odisha, Bihar, West Bengal, undivided Madhya Pradesh, Chhattisgarh, and Jharkhand before rising to a senior position at the time of retirement. It is but natural that he could write with credibility about the men who run the rails. With an insider's keen eyes and being privy to the backroom dealings, he could depict with deftness the real-life characters serving the railways—from the humble porter to the General Manager. His portrayal of the ordinary workers of the railways, who rise to the call of duty or even go beyond, is a tribute to the common man.

Out of his vast repertoire of railway related fiction, a novel and eleven short stories have been selected for this translation. The novel is an abridged version of the original, while the short stories contain the full translation. The novel *A Station Named Liligumma* (*Station Ra Na Liligumma*) is set in a period when the construction of a rail line was in progress. It is a narrative of how the railways made an inroad into an inaccessible territory. Out of the additions to the total rail line in the country, post-independence, two main rail lines stand out: Kottavalasa-Kirandul (KK) Rail Line (448 kilometres) and Koraput-Rayagada (KR) Rail Line (174 kilometres). Both the lines running through undivided Koraput district in Odisha, with its inaccessible mountain range and dense forest cover, are engineering marvels in themselves. For the novel, the author has chosen the ecosystem of the KR Rail line as the backdrop. The station "Liligumma", nestled in the hills of Koraput is the theatre where the story unfolds.

As regards the short stories, Shri Sahoo has crafted them with irony and subtle humour. In "Draupadi", the protagonist tears away the façade of the urban gentry, in "Big Boss", help comes from unexpected quarters. The "Serpent" story is about the eternal conflict between love and lust while "Casabianca" is about the surreal bond between man and animal. Shri Sahoo's gentle humour comes out in stories like "Complaint" and "Pomeranian". In the mix, are suspense and crime stories as well, such as "Ghost of Bhanwartonk" and "Tiger Hill files."

For the translator, translating the stories from Odia to English was itself like a train journey. At a time when train journeys are being increasingly replaced with air trips, the human drama unfolding on and off the railway tracks will hopefully make for a fascinating read. The translator's efforts will be rewarded if the stories strike a chord in the heart of the readers.

-Malabika Patel

A Station Named Liligumma

1

Is it the same Dandakaranya, whose description in the *Ramayana* was so hair-raising? As a child, Srikant had, in his mind, created grisly images of this very forest. Now, many years later, he found himself standing on a small hilltop in the same Dandakaranya, amazed, his eyes savouring the scenic view. Above him was the azure sky, stretching towards the horizon; all around were the undulating hills; where one ended, the other began, laden with vegetation and standing together like motionless devotees, as if revering the Creator. The morning sun shone brightly on their faces.

Countless trees and plants were all around. Srikant could barely estimate how many. From time immemorial, man has been worshipping them as gods. Being brought up in the village, he could recognize some of the trees—sal, piasal, asan, kurum, arjun—but many he could not.

It was springtime in Dandakaranya. The trees had donned various shades: green, orange, copper; the mango trees were sporting bunches of flowers. The aroma of the mahul trees was floating in the air, and from a distance, a flowering shimli tree resembled a proud jungle rooster.

Srikant looked up to find a huge tree in front of him. It was hugged by a scrounger of a creeper. Laden with red flowers, it was happily sponging off the tree like a brazen maiden. A serene silence pervaded. The mild morning breeze was gently sweeping the foliage, the leaves murmuring as if in a secret conversation with each other. A few birds flew away chirping in search of food.

The tranquillity of the forest was like a thirst-quenching drink. Srikant had always been a worshipper of silence, even in his childhood. Standing atop the hill, he felt like drinking cups full of it. It reminded him of the peace of the jungle in his village, once the showpiece of the same village. The jungle had been full of fruit-bearing trees: jamun, amla, kendu, besides sal, sissoo, teak, and other timber-giving trees. It was a happy hunting ground for animals like the deer, boar, mouse-deer, rabbit, monkeys, mongoose, along with birds like the peacock, woodpecker, hoopoe, quail, and more. Even tigers were said to have roamed long ago, as recounted by his grandfather. But courtesy of British predators, they had vanished by the time he had grown up. As a kid, Srikant remembered wandering around the fringes of the jungle, climbing its numerous fruit-bearing trees, and settling into picnics with his friends on its grassy meadows. When the village road gave way to a national highway, the jungle lost its sheen; it was stripped naked. The trees fell to the greed of the timber mafia. The hills skirting the jungle were then blasted for chips by the stone crusher merchants, and their remnants had looked like the skeletons of prehistoric dinosaurs.

Will the same fate fall upon the pristine forests of Dandakaranya? Srikant had come to Dandakaranya as an engineer while working for the Indian Railways. He would be part of the laying of a railway line in this virgin hilly area. He wondered what would happen when the rail lines would tear into this sylvan forest cover? The same thing that happened to his village jungle? The giant machines that would come to lay the lines would blast dynamite, conquer the virgin mountains and drill tunnels into them. Concrete and steel bridges would wrap the green valley. The gorgeous, sentinel-like trees would be felled to make room for swanky stations, and localities would spring up around it. The utilitarian needs of the growing human population would then take over. Industries would be set up to excavate the rich minerals stored in the womb of mother earth; mine owners, traders, contractors, industrialists … all would swoop down on the place, and new human settlements would spring up from nowhere. What would happen to the original inhabitants of the place who have lived alongside nature, protected the flora and fauna, the varied wildlife and their motherland, for centuries? Will the so-called "uncivilized tribals" be ousted by the so-called "resource-hungry civilised"?

Srikant had no answer. *Should I be a part of this process of transformation or should I abdicate my responsibility?* He was in a dilemma. He remembered his history lessons. Like civilizations that had sprung up on the banks of rivers, industrialization happened with the advent of the railways, and the standard of living increased manifold for the people inhabiting the sites. Railways would bring development in education, health, and agriculture in this underdeveloped region.

Leaning against his jeep, Srikant was lost in the debate of "development versus preservation". He was clueless as to whether "development" was good for the people or not. One voice told him not to be an agent of destructive creation, the other wanted him to be a catalyst for development. Maybe the inhabitants themselves needed a change, he supposed. He was a mere junior engineer, a paid employee of the rail department; the hierarchy above him and the powers-that-be would decide where the tracks would be laid. It was not for him to debate the pros-and-cons of it, but simply to carry out the orders. He was there reporting at Liligumma camp for the construction of Koraput-Rayagada rail line. That was it.

A bird flew overhead and called as if telling him, "Go back, go back. Do not rob us of our habitat."

The sun rose high. With his pair of binoculars, he tried to look far. He could see three white-water streams tumbling down from a precipice and falling on to a rock below. He thought of going near the waterfall. Negotiating the slopes, he came down to a valley where some tribal women were bending down on the field with shovels. They wore colourful saris that only reached above their knees, and their hair was knotted in a one-sided bun. He wanted to go near them. But the lines of the poem "The Solitary Reaper," which he had read during his high-school days, flashed in his mind:

> "Behold her, single in the field,
> Yon solitary highland lass!
> Reaping and singing by herself
> Stop here or gently pass."

Srikant let them be.

❖ ❖ ❖

2

Srikant had cleared the competitive entrance exam for the All India Engineering Services. He got Indian Railways, which was his first choice. His mother, however, was not exactly happy. A teacher's job near the village would have ensured proximity to her future daughter-in-law and grandchildren. That was her refrain. She was a widow and Srikant her only child. An enthusiastic Srikant assured her that he would come to the village every month and also take her around—from Kashmir to Kanyakumari, courtesy the Indian Railways.

"Won't you like to see Mathura and Vrindavan?" Srikant had asked.

"No, Son. This village is my Mathura, my Vrindavan. I have no interest in going anywhere," was her teary reply.

Training in Pune completed, Srikant was asked to report to the General Manager (GM), South Eastern Railway, Kolkata. Suited-booted, he reached the GM's office. The GM's office was situated at Garden Reach. The three-storeyed building, built in an Indo-Saracenic style, was once the property of Wajid Ali Shah of Awadh, later purchased by Bengal Nagpur Railway (BNR) from his descendants.

With his joining letter in hand, Srikant was pacing up and down the corridor, when white-uniformed peons directed him to the Secretary of the GM. The Secretary's head was buried under a mountain of files, some of which he was browsing and some he was throwing down. Peons were being summoned to carry away the files, while Srikant kept standing in attention.

When he lifted his head and uttered, "Yes?" Srikant showed him his joining letter, upon which he again pressed the bell to tell the peon to take him to the Chief Personnel Officer (CPO's) office.

At the CPO's office in the same building, he was taken by another peon to the private secretary of the CPO, who, on seeing the letter, directed him to meet the Deputy Chief Personnel Officer (Gazetted).

The Dy CPO (Gaz) had not reached the office, though it was already 11a.m. His peon explained that he had to take a train to Howrah from his downtown residence and then reach the office by bus—no mean task. Srikant could wait inside his chamber. It was a favour, which the peon made him realize.

Finally, the Dy CPO (Gaz) arrived in a huff and was surprised to see a visitor inside his chamber. He darted questions at Srikant.

"Who are you?"

Srikant revealed his identity.

To the peon, "Was Bada Sahib looking for me?"

"No, Sir."

"Take this gentleman to the gazetted section head clerk, Pal Babu."

Srikant followed the peon to the third floor.

"This is his seat," said the peon and left.

Srikant's query about the occupant—Pal Babu—elicited the usual response from the neighbouring clerk: "Dada! Work doesn't happen like this. People come from as far as Kharagpur, Sealdah, Chitpur. Go and take a round outside. They will, of course, come."

A befuddled Srikant did not know where to take a round. A trip to the washroom would just kill some time; it was not a matter of urgency. He took off his tie and jacket, and kept it neatly in his attaché. When he got back to the hall, a pair of spectacles and a bag had made an appearance on the table, suggesting Pal Babu's arrival.

Soon, a bespectacled and short man with a water bottle in hand came to occupy the chair and asked for his customary tea from the tea boy.

Then he looked at Srikant and his letter. "I will prepare the note and send it to the Chief Engineer (CE). You may come after lunch."

What to do with himself till lunchtime? Srikant was clueless. He sauntered around and came to the back of the building. And lo! The Hooghly River was flowing in all its majesty. On the other side of the river, one could see the huge expanse of the botanical garden. A Kali mandir and a bench completed the scene. Srikant sat on the bench, witnessing the spirited flow of the river, assured of its final destination nearby.

In contrast, he was anxious. He knew not of his posting.

It was finally lunchtime. Srikant got up, but instead of heading to the office dining room—where liveried attendants served the officers a full-course lunch on round tables lined with shining cutlery—he had lunch at the roadside eatery, which displayed a signboard of rice and fish curry for "Rs 5/- only".

Back at the desk, Pal Babu said, "Your file has gone to the CE. He will decide your posting. Then the office order will come out."

It was almost late afternoon when he finally managed to enter the cabin of the CE.

Bending with a bow, he offered his salutation. "I am Srikant Das, Probationary Engineer."

"Please sit down," said a baritone voice. "I have given orders for your posting at Adra Division."

Srikant's face fell.

"What—are you not happy with this posting?"

"Sir, is there no vacancy in Khurda Road Division?"

"You seem to be homesick, young man! All officers of your state are like this. When you join an all-India service, how can you ask for a posting near your hometown?" He paused. "Listen to me," he added, guardian-like, "do not go there. People there have a habit of complaining about their officers, instead of working. Are you scared of the law-and-order situation in Adra?"

"Yes, Sir."

"Okay. Then I will send you to Waltiar instead. Good division. People are simple, and your training will be done amidst the mountains, rivers, forest, and mines."

"Thank you, Sir," Srikant smiled.

By the time of the drafting of the joining letter, its verification, typing, and signing were completed, it was 6 in the evening.

Srikant rushed towards Howrah station.

3

The Railway Ministry had appointed Rail India Technical & Economic Services limited (RITES) to conduct a survey of the two routes, Koraput–Rayagada and Koraput–Parvatipuram. When the report was published in 1982, heavy lobbying by the two states involved—Odisha and Andhra Pradesh—commenced. RITES had suggested a direct line between Koraput and Rayagada, instead of Koraput–Parvatipuram (in Andhra Pradesh) because of the heavy gradient in the latter section. The report stated that the former alignment had plenty of bauxite nearby. L&T and Indian Aluminium Co. were interested in opening aluminium plants near Kewtaguda and Tikri. The Railway Board, therefore, decided in favour of Koraput Rayagada (KR) Line.

The Traffic Survey also highlighted the benefits of the proposed new line.

First, the biggest iron ore deposit at Bailadila in Bastar district of Madhya Pradesh supplied hematite iron ore to Vishakhapatnam port, to be exported to China and Japan via Kottavalasa Kirandul (KK) line, which was completed in 1968. The KR Line, if built, would serve as a bypass. Second, for the biggest aluminium refinery at Damanjodi, the KR line would act as a feeder and the distance between Damanjodi and the smelter plant at Angul would be reduced. Third, the rich reserve of limestone, bauxite, graphite, carbide, and forest produce of Koraput and Rayagada district could be tapped into for rapid growth of the area, with the help of a railway line. Fourth, a railway line amidst the scenic beauty of the hills, mountains, valleys, and forest in the area could boost tourism and make tourist spots like Gupteswar, Sabar Srikshetra, Duduma falls,

Sunabeda, Jalaput, Nandapur more attractive and popular.

The proposed rail line was to be built in a mountainous range, which called for the expertise of capable engineers. Only committed engineers were asked to apply for deputation in the project. Many showed little interest in this godforsaken area.

However, Srikant accepted the challenge.

4

As far as possible, railway tracks are aligned away from habitation and cultivated land, mainly to reduce the cost of compensation. The most difficult thing, however, was clearing forests and felling trees in protected forests, which required environmental clearance.

The first day at the site, Srikant took some labour and employees to clear a relatively less dense jungle. While at work, he suddenly sensed a bush shaking and a pair of eyes watching them from behind the bush. First, he thought it must be some wild animal. But then he saw a head from behind the trees, popping up and down like a chameleon. After some time, the scantily clad figure with a spear in hand got up from behind the bush and crawled away, down the hills.

A bit later, he heard the sound of madal drums and singa. The sound grew louder as a dozen tribal folks, with two elderly persons, came menacingly close to them. The workers left their work and stood stupefied.

Srikant cautioned the workers, "They consider us the enemy, perhaps. All of you … stand quiet." He then asked the tribal head, "What is the matter?"

The tribal leader wore headgear; a loincloth covered his lower torso. A six-feet pole was in his hand. Others had bows and arrows and spears in their hands. Waving the pole, the leader gesticulated, as if asking them to come with him.

"But where?" Srikant was taken aback. He explained that they were railway people and were harmless. Meanwhile, the driver had started the jeep in panic, when an arrow struck it. Srikant shouted at him to not do such irresponsible things. "These folks seem aggressive. Don't invite trouble." He asked the driver to stop the jeep's engine and join them.

The tribals then tied up each of the labourers with siyali creepers and directed them to follow the chieftain. The workers were shaking in fear, but Srikant reassured them. "There is nothing to be scared of. The tribals are suspicious that strangers will take possession of their hills and forests. Have patience." Similar incidents had taken place when the Kottavalasa–Kirandul line was being built. The tribals were opposing the building of a rail line.

The workers, along with Srikant, moved in a line, with the tribal head leading them. Behind were the other tribals, with their spears and drum beaters.

Srikant was reminded of the stories he had heard at Baroda Staff College during his foundation course training. To keep the workers' morale high, he kept recounting to them, how even in England there was a stiff protest against the laying of rail lines. The Duke of Cumberland, Queen Victoria's uncle, had opined that the sound of the Great Eastern Railway would derange the school children of Eton, antisocial people would spread far and wide, cows would stop lactating, and trees would stop bearing fruit in areas where the rail line would pass. Such stories kept the captive workers amused.

Finally, they reached the tribal hamlet, which had a huge banyan tree in the middle and a shrine for their God underneath. The houses of the Kondh tribals were lined in two neat rows.

Hearing the sound of the drums, people from the huts came rushing towards the tree. Srikant noticed, most women worn cotton saris that went up to their knees, had heavy ornaments dangling from their noses, trinkets on their necks, while the men had a loincloth on them. The children were in their birthday suits, a single talisman on the waist. Some women had suckling babies strapped to their bodies.

Hearing the noise, a young lady in her early twenties came out of a nearby room. She was clad in a simple sari—no ornaments but a fresh and bright face, as if the Goddess Saraswati herself had come out of a tapestry. Seeing the tied-up workers, she shot a question at the chieftain in the Kui language, "Why have you got them here all tied up?"

"These people have come with their vehicle and guns... will take away our girls and children," Jani Budha, the chieftain replied.

The lady then asked Srikant, "Who are you, and why you all have come here?"

"We are railway people. A new rail line is coming into this area. We are working to build it."

"Yes, I have heard. But these people fear that you will take away their children in your vehicles."

Srikant smiled.

"Okay, wait. Let me explain to them," she said.

"*Ninu train hindanji. Aditundi lamba lahagadi. Maa nayunti sabu loku a gadita jagiliadinilu. Godatani jaka besi hadane.* (Have you not seen a train, Jani Budha? It is a long iron cart. All the people can sit in that cart. It runs faster than a horse.)"

"*Astiki begi?* (Stronger than an elephant?)"

The lady smiled. "*Karnitiki jaka besi hadane. Galitiki besi. Nana Raygadata hajiru. Embatia Cuttack, Bhubaneswar, Puri Jagannath dham. Mahapuru hendiru.* (Stronger than a tiger. At the speed of wind. I have seen the train at Raygada. If the train runs from here, you also can go to Raygada. From there to Cuttack, Bhubaneswar, and Puri Jagannath Dham. You can see Lord Jagannath.)"

"*No, No. Manayun pisyna ambia halagu. Maa chasa aasti beraha chintunu. Maheru dambilu mahajan aatuni.* (We will not go anywhere and leave our village. Our crops will be eaten away by elephants and wild boars. The Damba moneylender will capture the hamlet. Dharmu God will be angry.)"

"*Train waten cihakiri medayen. Jadasuda rejili aeye. Mi kakaru babu aniru. Mile airu lenfgti hochana recehen aji hatene?* (When the train comes, you all will get jobs. You don't have to roam in the jungles. Your children will be babus. Will you like them to roam like you in a loincloth?)"

The old man still had doubts. "*Emba company tax lagwaye ta?* (Will this company impose tax?)"

"*Aye. Aye tax lagwaye. Midi sabu ajine. Minge jinish patar docahan ajile aye. Ropga ati lokun daktar khanas dekana ahili aye. E uron pistudiu. E waru sarakari babu. Nahele police wahanga minge gaspa ayaniru.* (No. No tax will be imposed. Rather, you will not have to walk with your luggage on your head. Your sick people will not be carried in makeshift stretchers to the hospital. Free these people. They are *sarkari* people. If you don't, Daroga Babu will take you away.)"

The chieftain understood. He knew the Daroga Babu well.

"*Hade kakaru. Ae worun pistadu.* (Yes, children. Free them.)"

The village folks also understood.

The lady spoke to Srikant, "These people are all scared of the Forester, the Daroga, the Revenue Inspector and other officers. For years, they have been exploited by such people. They come and extract their savings in the name of tax, catch their fowl, goat, and other pets for their feasts. Sometimes they flirt with the girls. That is why they are highly suspicious of any outsiders."

"Many thanks for your help, Madam. But for you, we don't know what would have happened," Srikant said and left the place with his team.

5

The labour contractors brought labourers from Hyderabad, Madhya Pradesh, and Ganjam district of Odisha. Mud huts with tin-roofs sprang up along the proposed rail line. The landless Oda tribals from Hyderabad were known for their expertise in mud work. Even Chhattisgarhi farm labourers from Madhya Pradesh were hardworking, but they worked only during their off-season. The local labour force was still shy of offering their services. Language was a stumbling block.

Srikant needed an interlocutor. In a flash, he remembered the schoolteacher, Kumudini, who had saved his team from the assault.

Driving to the tribal hamlet where the school was situated was easy now. Srikant sought her assistance as an interpreter to mobilize labour. Kumudini readily agreed and promised to make it there on a Sunday.

The drive to Kakudipadar, a Kondh village, was a long one. "I am so happy, Kumudini Madam, that you have agreed to help us."

"Please don't call me 'Madam'; call me Kumud instead. You are doing such good work for our area. I will be proud if I can be of any help. But tell me … the hilly range is continuous here. One starts where the other ends. How will the train move on these hills? Will it not fall down?"

Srikant smiled. "Tunnels will be made to make way into the hills. A total of thirty-six tunnels will be made."

"But how will you join the valleys?"

"Viaducts or bridges will be constructed. Seventy-seven big bridges are proposed. The number of small bridges will be more than three hundred and fifty."

"All these will take many years then."

"Yes, it will take at least three to four years to construct this line. Dynamite will blast through the hills, the big boulders will be carried by cranes, labourers will help to carry boulders and earth."

"You need big contractors; here there are only petty ones."

"Oh, yes."

True enough, they sighted a coolie sardar on the side of the road, taking a roll call of the coolies present. Srikant stopped his jeep. The sardar was calling out the names of the coolies one by one.

"Sambari!"

One coolie raised his hand and said, "Hazari."

Sardar called out another name, "Sania!"

"Budhia," responded another coolie and went to the other side. Now, it was the turn of a Reza coolie.

"Sajani!"

In response, one woman got up, covered her mouth with her pallu, and with a giggle went over to the other side.

"What kind of a roll call is this? Why are the coolies responding in different names?" Kumud asked.

Srikant laughed. "It is so different from your school roll call, na? Kids must be saying 'Yes, Miss' or 'Present, Madam' when you call out their names. But here, in the railways, the response is to take your father's or husband's name."

"Why so?"

"Because most of the names of the coolies are similar; the only differentiating factor is the father's or husband's name."

"Indeed, that is funny!"

Soon, they reached the village of Kakudipadar, of the Kondh tribes.

"I have heard of Meria human sacrifice by the Kondhs," Srikant mumbled.

"That was during the British regime. Legend has it that on a terrible drought year, an old Kondh was so miserable looking at the cloudless sky and parched land that God Dharani Penu took pity on him. A voice from the sky said, 'God is angry with you. Unless you satiate him with blood, everything will be destroyed.' From that day onwards, a man is waylaid, fed well, and on the day of puja, tied up to the 'Meri'. The kondhs then circle around him, intoxicated on mahul brew, and dance wild to the beat of madal drums and singa. Finally, Jani beheads the captive with a machete, and the blood is then offered to God."

"Such a savage practice. Have you witnessed it?"

"No, it has been banned long since. Now they practise an animal sacrifice instead. They sacrifice hens, pigs, and goats as offerings to Dangar Penu."

"But are they industrious?"

"The women are. They forage the forest for wood, sal leaves, grass for brooms, roots, berries, fruits, and more, and also work in the hutments. Once, the Kondh tribals were fierce and brave. Even the British government had got a taste of their penchant for guerrilla war."

The village looked deserted. Only the headman of the village was sitting in a spot, like an anthill. A dog sat by his side.

"*Juhar budha Jani*," Kumud paid her salutations.

"*Embaya railway kama chal wahane, kunjaliru*? (Railway work is going on here. Do you know?)"

"*Han kunjai.* (Yes, I know.)"

"*Railway ta loku darker. Nikakaruun pandadu. Besi lebuun medayanu. Barsasara dina majuri medayanu.* (The Railway needs people. Will you send your folks? They will get good money. Throughout the year.)"

"*Ae ni kama kinuru?* (What work will they do?)"

"*Wiria ualaka kandiru.* (They will lift stones and mud.)"

"*Ae ni kama kinuru? Ewaruun daadayyu perihi perihi weda hache. Yangata badiumane* (What work will these people do? All the time they are behind the *dhangdis.* Do they have the strength?)"

Srikant and Kumud broke into smiles. Srikant said, "They will get good money."

"*Achaka majuri hiyaniru?* (How much money will they get?)"

"Males will get fifty rupees, females twenty," Kumud explained.

"*Han han nanu wesayain.* (I will tell them.)"He bowed his head and went back to his stupor.

"Tell them to meet contractor Harish Babu at Liligumma," Srikant said and started the jeep. On the way back, he suggested Kumud have a look at his camp.

"You stay for days in this forest," Kumud said. "Must be a difficult life for you."

"Yes, but much more difficult is the gangman's life. They are the foot soldiers of the railways. Come rain, storm or sunshine, they are the ones ensuring the security of the rail tracks. They are exposed to attacks of wild animals; many even die of snake bites. But they are the lowest in the hierarchy of the railways."

Srikant continued, "Have you heard of that event—in Uganda-Kenya? Towards the end of the nineteenth century, when the British Railways was building a bridge on river Tsavo, hundred and forty labourers became victims to a pair of man-eating lions within a period of nine months."

"Yes, I have also read a story in high school. *Tiger in the Tunnel.*

The work of the gangmen is indeed dangerous and difficult," replied Kumud.

The jeep had reached Liligumma camp. Under the sal thickets, where sunlight could hardly penetrate, four Swiss tents were put up. One was for Srikant, two for his employees, and one was folded up as a kitchen-cum-dining room. Srikant's tent had a drawing-room, a bedroom, and a toilet.

The natty layout was a surprise for Kumud. "It really looks like a war camp belonging to some emperor."

"Have lunch here, Kumud."

"No, Sir. I have to go back home."

Srikant had never been so free with any woman. In the village, there was no scope; in college, he was shy. In Kumud's presence, he felt a strange delight, but he could hardly express it. He felt like singing to her the lines of an old Hindi song:

"*Abhi abhi toh ayi ho, bahar banke chhayi ho … Abhi na jao chodkar, ke dil abhi bhara nahi!* (You have just come, bringing spring to my life! Stay back, na, for some more time; I am not yet done.)"

But the words got lost on the way to his mouth. He could only instruct his driver to drop Kumud off.

6

Deputy Chief Engineer (Construction), Arindam Ghosh was Srikant's immediate boss. Always homesick for Kolkata and with an abiding interest in cricket, for which he used to make a trip to the city every month, he was finding his posting in the KR line a punishment to the core. Being a direct recruit himself, he had a soft corner for Srikant and let him have a lot of operational freedom. The other two AENs, Rama Rao and Padmanabhan, were promotee officers. But he never discriminated against them and gave them an equal degree of freedom.

"Sir, the jungle has been cleared," Srikant reported.

"Did the District Forest Officer (DFO) create any problem?"

"No, Sir."

Labour contractor Harishchandra was asked, "When will you start the work?"

"Sir, the labourers have come. Srikant Sir has mobilized labour roaming around the nearby villages. Work will start on Wednesday."

The other two AENs reported about their respective areas of work. Arindam Ghosh gave instructions while winding up his review meeting: "Now, it is the beginning of April. Earthwork should finish by June-end. July-August-September will be months of heavy rain. Work has to stop. After that, compacting work will start. Hope all of you understand."

"Yes, Sir," his subordinates said in unison.

❖ ❖ ❖

7

After his coronation, King Yayati Keshari of Kalinga of the tenth century had brought ten thousand Brahmins from Kanyakubja to his kingdom for the purpose of performing horse sacrifice ceremony on the banks of river Baitarani. In the coastal areas, he had made a large number of land grants to the Brahmins and built temples whose upkeep was handed over to them. Several centuries later, the Brahmins spread to various parts of Odisha in search of livelihood.

Western Odisha was the choice of Gajanan Mishra. Koraput, with a predominantly tribal population, had few Hindu temples, as tribal Gods were different from Hindu Gods. Out of the few, he was the priest of a Shiv temple located in the foothills of Liligumma.

Gajanan Mishra had one son and three daughters; the son had joined the Indian Army, while the other two sisters, Pankajini and Kallolini, were matriculates and in search of jobs. Kumudini was a graduate with B.Ed. degree and was employed as a teacher in Sikarpai primary school. The primary school had only two teachers with no Headmistress to boot, as the tribal area was an avoidable posting for many. Kumud had to double as the Headmistress.

Most of the students in the school belonged to the tribal community. The rest belonged to lower castes. More than sitting in the classroom, roaming in the jungle and hunting small game, appeared more alluring to the students. To reduce absenteeism, Kumud had to devise ways, sometimes counselling the parents, at times bribing the kids with biscuits and chocolates with her own money, telling stories. Extracurricular activities like sports, drawing, painting, handicraft were given more emphasis than bookish knowledge. No wonder she was a popular figure in the village.

One afternoon, when the final bell was about to ring, she asked the children, "Would you all like to go for a picnic, children?"

A chorus followed. "Yes, Miss."

"Where would you like to go?"

Everyone looked at each other. They had no clue where to go.

"Have you seen Gupteswar?"

"No," was the chorus.

"Okay, we will go to Gupteswar."

The excited chatter of the children could be heard while Kumud boarded the Raygada-Tikri bus, her regular mode of transport for commuting from her village.

8

Next day, Kumud was found at the rail line site where Srikant was supervising.

"Sir, does your railway have a bus?"

"Why a bus?"

"I am thinking of taking my children to Gupteswar for a picnic. They need to go out of the classroom and learn."

"Yes, that is a good idea. We don't have a bus, but it can be arranged. But on one condition."

"What is the condition?"

"You have to take this student along. I also need to enhance my knowledge of Koraput."

Both of them laughed. "Okay, you come along as well."

"Then one more condition, since you have agreed to the first one. I will arrange breakfast for all."

"Arre! You seem to have a large heart."

"No, my chest size is only thirty-six inches."

One more round of combined laughter.

The next Sunday, early in the morning, Srikant started making arrangements for the picnic party. He ensured the loading of cooking utensils in his jeep. One peon and an inspector accompanied him. The jeep was used as an advance party. At Koraput bus stand, sixty packets of snacks had to be loaded, the inspector was instructed.

The bus was to follow. Kumud did a headcount while the excited children bade goodbye to their parents who had come to see them off. Another teacher, a cook and his helper, boarded the bus.

Srikant and Kumud sat in the front row of the bus. The bus started moving and the kids started dozing. Srikant too followed suit. The early morning breeze wafting into the moving vehicle was enough to make him slip into his old habit. He was falling on Kumud, and kept getting up to mumble "sorry, sorry". This went on for some time, when Kumud finally shouted, "See, see! The ocean has caught fire!" Actually, the fire was on the shimli and palash trees. They were laden with flaming red flowers.

The sight was enough to wake Srikant up.

"Do you know why the name of this forest is Dandakaranya?" she asked him.

"Na! I don't have the faintest idea."

"According to the Puranas, a demon named Dandak ruled over this forest. This is the largest forest range in the country. Spreading over Andhra Pradesh, Bastar district of Madhya Pradesh, Koraput and Kalahandi district of Odisha, it has many famous rivers. The one famous in the Puranas is Tamasa, on the banks of which Maharshi Valmiki had his ashram. Here, he had composed his world-famous epic Ramayana."

"Really?"

"You don't believe me?"

"No...go on."

"Do you know the first poem of the world?"

"No."

"*Ma Nishad! Pratistham twamagam saswati sama. Yat krauncha mithunadekamabadhi kamamohitam.*" Her voice sounded more melodious when she recited it. "There is a legend behind this poem. Do you know it?"

Srikant knew it, but he said "no" and asked her to recount.

"One crane couple was playing on the branch of a tree. Maharshi Valmiki was going for his bath to river Tamasa when he saw one of the birds fall from the branch, shot dead by an archer. The other bird kept circling around, wailing for its partner. The sloka was a spontaneous outpouring of sorrow by Maharshi Valmiki."

A brief silence followed. Then Kumud started, "Devi Sita was bathing in this river Tamasa. There is a big stone on its bank, where she used to scrub her feet."

"It seems you have seen Sita Mai bathing here."

They both shared a hearty laugh.

At Koraput bus stand, packets of snacks were loaded and distributed among the children.

"Let us get down and have a cup of tea," Srikant suggested.

"I don't take tea."

"But if I don't, I will again fall on you."

He got down and got two cups of tea, "Have it for my sake."

While crossing Ramgiri mountain, Kumud started, "Sri Ramchandra halted at this place during his exile. Hence the name."

"Any more legend behind it?" Srikant quipped.

"It is said that during Raja Vikramaditya's invasion, poet Kalidas had accompanied him. Fascinated by the beauty of this place, he stayed here and composed his epic poem, Meghadutam. Have you read it?"

"Sanskrit and me? I am dumb when it comes to the language. Somehow, I scraped through it in my school finals. I only remember *naraha narau naraa.*"

"What comes after that?"

"Piaji, pakoda, and baraa."

Both of them burst out laughing.

Srikant asked, "Have you read *Meghadutam*?"

"I am a student of Sanskrit. I had it as a subject in my graduation course."

"Then you are a pundit indeed. What had Kalidas written in Meghadutam?"

"It is the story of a Yaksha, a celestial being. He was banished from a kingdom called Alakapuri and was living a life of a recluse in Ramgiri. But he was absorbed in the thoughts about his beloved. He used to send messages to his beloved with the help of the clouds. The path that the clouds traversed in order to take his messages to his beloved is elaborately described in the epic poem. It was my favourite poem."

Meanwhile, the advance party had reached Gupteswar and cleared the site for their picnic. They even had lit the fire for cooking. The children alighted from the bus and were all gung-ho to explore. But they had to form a beeline, with Kumud leading and Srikant following her, on the narrow jungle pathway. Down the winding road, amidst sky-kissing trees, foliage hugging boulders with bird nests hanging among nooks and crannies, the line of children looked like a colourful train on a bend. Finally, they reached the sacred cave of Lord Gupteswar.

For a long time, Srikant and Kumud stood transfixed in front of the lingam. They offered water and flowers to the shrine. Down the cave was Saberi river, strewn with stones. Sitting on a stone, Srikant asked, "What did you ask God for?"

"Nothing. What did you ask for?"

Srikant wanted to say, I asked for your hand. Instead, he said, "I was reminded of the famous lines of saint-poet Bhima Bhoi, 'Let my life be in hell, but may the world get salvation.' So I said, 'Let the world be blessed.'"

Ha-ha! They laughed together. Kumud added, "Are you the saint-poet of the railways?"

"Only an obedient servant."

After they returned from Gupteswar and dropped the children off at the school, Srikant suggested, "Let me drop you home."

"Come to our poor house. I can only serve you tea."

"But you don't take tea."

"All at home take tea, except for me."

The jeep halted in front of Kumud's house. It was a modest brick house with a tiled roof. Srikant entered the house. The interior was simple, with a few belongings, but one shelf was crammed with books. English, Sanskrit, Odia—all types of books were vying for attention.

"So reading is your hobby," commented Srikant.

"And what is yours?"

"Binaca Geetmala on the radio and old Hindi songs."

"Excuse me," Kumud went inside.

Her sisters accosted her. "Who has accompanied you, Didi?" asked Pankajini.

"He is a railway engineer. He arranged a bus for the schoolchildren."

"Did he also accompany you for the picnic?" teased Kallolini.

Kumud broke into a smile "Yes." With a mild rebuke, she added, "Arre, will you make tea or keep interrogating me?"

Tea and biscuits were served. Kumud's mother and both her sisters joined them. They all were sizing up Srikant from head to foot. Srikant almost gulped the tea and said, "Auntie, let me leave."

After he left, Kumud became voluble in praise of Srikant. How he promptly agreed to arrange a bus, sponsored the breakfast and made all the arrangements for cooking with the help of his own staff. He even played with the children at Gupteswar.

Putting a brake on her raptures over Srikant, her mother asked, "What is his name?"

"Srikant Das."

"Is he a Brahmin Das or a low-caste Das? Did you ask him?"

"Is it something to ask, Maa? How long will you keep holding on to caste Maa?"

9

Come March, the mango trees decorate their tresses with flower beads. Palash, shimli—the trees wear bangles of flowers. Sal and piasal trees wear green saris. The cuckoo keeps on calling for his mate. His unrelenting musical note signs the arrival of spring. The silence of the forest is shattered by the coarse voice of the peacock. Only then do the tribal folk know that their Chaitra parab is not far. After months of hard work, the time for merrymaking has come.

Srikant woke up early in the morning to the incessant call of the cuckoo and the chirping of other birds, as if they were singing in a choir. He came out of his tent and stood mesmerized. All around, nature had left the spread that exists in a gallery: the azure sky, the lush green foliage, multicoloured flowers in full bloom, it seemed nature had flowered into a fully endowed, youthful woman. The youthful exuberance of nature resonated in him too. However, unlike nature, he realized it was a once-in-a-lifetime experience for human beings. To be young was exhilarating indeed. Under that heady feeling, his thoughts veered to Kumud. But he couldn't fathom why he was thinking of her so much? Was he attracted to her comely physical appearance or was she otherwise beautiful too?

He had never tasted the sentiments of romantic love. In the village, it was a forbidden topic. He had reconciled to the thought that he would experience such love only after his marriage. But why this sudden overwhelming feeling for her? And what is the future of such a sentiment?

Sitting on a chair in front of the tent, he wondered whether it will be in his fate to get such a beautiful girl like Kumud as a life-partner? She was true to her name; a white lily in a rocky hill. Her external behaviour would attract anyone, but whether she was good within too, he wondered.

How to know her mind? Certainly difficult to know what lies behind a woman's courteous behaviour.

"Sir, tea," Lembua's voice broke his musings. He continued to stand with folded hands.

"Tell me …"

"Sir, if you so hukum."

"Okay, tell."

"Have to go to the village, three days only, Sir."

"But you had gone only recently."

"That time my daughter was not well, Sir."

"What for will you go now?"

"Chaitra parab, Sir. My family will be waiting for me, Sir."

"For how many days?"

"Only three days."

"But don't make it ten days—like last time. And, don't drink too much, or your job will go."

"No Sahib, daru and me? Na ... never." He left, bending with gratitude.

Then came Hajari. Lembua was a Kondh, and while Hajari was not, he was clever and manipulative.

"Sahib, will go to village for Chaitra parab."

"Lembua is going. How can both of you go? Besides, you have no children."

"But I have a woman, Sahib."

"How many do you have?"

Srikant knew about his colourful nature.

"Swear, Sahib. Only one."

"Who will cook when you both leave?"

"Sahib, I have taught everything to Chhattisgarhi Hari Singh."

"Tell him to have my breakfast ready by eight. I have to go to the site."

Next day, Srikant's jeep halted at Kumud's school. Cleaning work in the school was going on. Kumud came to the gate.

"Sir, namskar. How is it that you are here?"

"I heard that preparations for the Chaitra festival are in full swing. Your school doesn't give chutti?"

"Only one day on purnima. But few students have come today."

"Then give the children chutti. You take me around na, to see your chaitra parab."

"No, Sir, I can't suspend the classes. If any supervisor comes, my job will be taken away."

"If they take away your job, I will give you one in the railways."

"Sir, please don't joke."

"Then shall I come tomorrow?"

"Yes, tomorrow is purnima. It will be good. This festival will go on for a month."

Srikant reversed his jeep. On the way, tribal folks were carrying new clothes and other goods. The migrant Dadan labourers were returning home with their belongings for the festival. Women with kids on their shoulders were returning to their father's house. Everywhere, there were signs of celebration. The hills were fragrant with mahul flowers and ready to welcome the revelry. The earthwork

of Liligumma-Raoli section would be delayed, Srikant apprehended.
But it could wait.

10

The chaitra festival had started with aplomb in Sikarpai village. The Kondh boys and girls were dancing under a banyan tree. The elders were sipping "salap" and watching the dance, while some of them were playing a variety of musical instruments.

The girls were wearing colourful saris, their oiled hair was tied in a lopsided bun, embellished with myriad beads; their ears, noses, necks, arms and waist, feet and toes, every inch had intricate ornaments like fine embroidery on fabric.

"So dressed up—from their nose to their nails," commented Srikant.

"Afterall, it is their festival (parab),"said Kumud.

Somebody held a drum, somebody held a mridang. Someone had a dungdunga, some a dhap. An array of instruments, a range of notes. But the melody that came from the instruments was like a symphony from an orchestra, albeit a rustic one. Swaying their hips in rhythm with the melody, hand in hand, shoulder brushing against shoulder, step matching step, the young girls were going round and round in a circle to the musical beat, dancing away to glory. From their lips were flowing the endless songs of a chorus.

"Sir, the songs that are being sung are called 'Kindri' songs."

"What is the meaning of Kindri?"

"Dancing in circles is called Kindri in the Kui language."

"Is any God worshipped in this Chaitra Parab?"

"The Chaitra Parab is for 'dumas'(ancestors') blessings."

One old woman came to them in a bent posture. "Hey you, Miss Teacher! Who is this person? Is he your husband?"

Srikant noticed Kumud's face turned red in embarrassment. She said with a laugh, "No, no. He is the Railway Sahib. He has come to see your dance."

"Sahib! Will you dance with us?"

Both Srikant and Kumud laughed, "Mausi you dance, we will enjoy watching it."

"Sir! Please give them some token money."

"Why, is it for salap?"

"Yes, take it that way."

Srikant took out a hundred rupee note and gave it to the old woman. The old woman waved the note in circles around Srikant's head and went back to join the dance.

Some girls came rushing to Kumud and dragged her to the mud dance floor.

Kumud stood coyly in the midst of the girls and made a step or two along with them.

While returning from the Parab, the sound of a cuckoo was heard but it was coarse; not like her usual sweet note. Srikant asked, "Why is the cuckoo sounding so coarse?"

Kumud broke into a laugh. The dimple in her cheek made her face shine with an incomparable gloss.

"Why did you laugh?"

"The cuckoo must be looking for a mate. This is their season for mating."

"Oh," Srikant laughed along.

"Sir! Who all are there in your family?"

"My widowed mother in the village."

"Why do you ask?"

"Just like that."

He asked the driver to drop Kumud off at her house. While she was taking his leave, a grateful look crossed his face. He wanted to say, "Thank you Kumud, for the experience of Chaitra parab," but the words escaped his lips.

The sound of mridang and dungdunga was reverberating throughout the camp. Srikant's heart resonated with it and sleep vanished from his eyes.

11

Rayagada Guest House had an air of briskness. The Chief Engineer (CE) had come from Garden Reach to take stock of the situation. The Chief Engineer (Construction) was to join him. All arrangements of hospitality, food, the presenting of mementoes and so on had been entrusted to the contractors.

The KR line map was spread out on the table. Pouring on it after a sumptuous breakfast was the CE. The CE (Con) and Dy CE (Con) were in attendance.

Arindam Ghosh, Dy CE (Con), introduced his two Assistant Engineers (AEN) and their respective contractors to the CE.

"Rayagada-Bhalumaska station, AEN Rama Rao and Contractor Sardar Gurusaran Singh."

"Bhalumaska-Tikri section, AEN Srikant Das and Contractor Harishchandra Baral."

"Tikri-Koraput section; AEN Padmanabhan and Contractor Harihar Sethia."

The CE (Con) reviewed the progress report. Arindam reported, "The forest has been cleared from Rayagada to Bhaumaska. The local DFO was creating problems. But an understanding has been reached. This section will have ten tunnels and twelve big bridges."

"Okay. Next."

"Bhalumaska-Tikri section has also been cleared of its forest. Srikant's liaising with the DFO helped matters. About twenty five per cent of the civil work has been completed. This section will have sixteen tunnels and ten big bridges."

"So, no problem in this section?"

"No, there was a problem with labour. But Srikant has toured the tribal area and scouted for labour in the name of the railways."

"Good."

"In the Tikri-Koraput section, civil earthwork has started, after clearing the jungle. This will have four tunnels and two major bridges. The estimate has been sent. Only the tendering remains."

The review over, three jeeps were kept ready for visiting the section. The three AENs got into one jeep.

"Call the young AEN to my jeep. Let me know how much he has learnt," said the CE. Srikant shifted to the CE's jeep.

"How is this young man performing?"

"Good Sir, but he is very soft," Arindam Ghosh replied with a smile.

"Oh, is that the case? Being soft will not work, young man. Railway work is very hard. You have to be tough. The railways work smoothly since the time of the British because of their toughness. Our people are basically lazy. One has to wield the whip. Of course, after Independence, we can't brandish the whip. But you have to be a firebrand and shout at people to get the work done."

"Okay, Sir," Srikant smiled shyly.

"Sir, the service roads are in a very pitiable condition. But the state government is playing deaf to our requests," informed Arindam Ghosh.

"The state governments have a step-motherly attitude towards the railways. They demand royalty even for earth removed."

"We will not cater to the state government's demands. You tell the contractor to quote keeping in mind the road condition, its distance from the track, etc. We cannot depend on the state government."

"Sir, one more problem. Because of the gulf war, the price of diesel has shot up. Contractors have stopped working because it is not available."

"Okay, on my return to headquarters, I will send an oil tank wagon to Rayagada and Koraput Depots."

"We will be thankful, Sir."

The jeep halted at Bhalumaska. Some labourers were working there.

"Rama Rao, your work is slow. No excuses. The work has to be completed within one month. Monsoon is approaching. Do you follow?"

"I will try, Sir," Rama Rao meekly said.

The next halt was at Liligumma.

"Sir, in this section, tunnels have to be built within a distance of one kilometre each. Local contractors cannot do the job. Big companies will participate in the tender, surely."

"Yes. Tender notice has been given. Before it commences, cutting and embankment work has to be completed," instructed the CE.

Lunch was arranged at Liligumma.

"Have you studied the topography of this place, Srikant?" the CE asked.

"Yes, Sir. I have read the GSI and Andhra University Report, Sir. Most of the land is composed of khandelite and quartz stones. The GSI report suspects slope failure, heavy seepage of water and over-break problems in this area."

"Good. Then conduct boring on a trial basis in the marked places and send the report."

12

It was early in the morning and black clouds in the western sky had started to move in a troupe, like pilgrims on a pilgrimage. When they were tired, they stopped and formed a huddle. The birds flew from tree to tree with their warning calls—"rains are not far away". Excitement ran through the leaves, the grasses and the shrubs, as if a welcome guest was on the way.

Srikant was awake, watching the tiptoeing of the changing season. The dark clouds reminded him of Kumud's description of Meghadutam, the story of lovelorn Yaksha and the Yakshini.

Rains remind one of their near and dear ones. His village was far away. He thought that a visit to his friend, Sachidanand, and his organization, Agradoot, would feel like a home away from home.

Sachidanand, Srikant's classmate at Ravenshaw College, Cuttack, was running an NGO by the name of Agradoot at Kusunpur village.

He drove to the village and located the office of Agradoot.

"Can I come in?" standing at the door, Srikant announced.

"Do you recognize me—Srikant Das, Ravenshaw West Hostel?"

"Oh. Yes, of course. I had heard of your joining the Railway Engineering Services."

"Yes. I have come to oversee Koraput-Rayagada line work."

"That is great indeed."

"Come, come. Sit down, this is a real surprise. Let us have tea."

"Kalpana! Bring two cups of nice ginger tea. The Railway officer has come. He will give us jobs in the Railway," Sachidanand shouted, then asked. "How far has the line progressed?"

"Just started."

"But this will not have a good impact on the tribal culture," Sachidanand quipped.

"Why? What is wrong if industries are set up and the mines are used? People will get employment."

"Please don't misunderstand Srikant, industries are good where the land is not put to agricultural use. Don't take away the land of the tribals. If you cut trees for your rail line, you have to afforest later. But not with eucalyptus, babool, acacia, and sumeria trees. Our organization is working for the preservation of the forest, among many other things."

"What else are you doing, Sachi?"

"We are collecting forest produce through our mahila samitis and directly selling it, instead of going through the middleman. A particular type of grass is being used for high-quality brooms, which are selling country-wide."

"Okay, tell me will your rail line go through this village Kusunpur?" Sachidanand continued.

"No."

"Then there is a nearby village called Liligumma. Can it go through that place?"

"This KR Line will have twelve stations. Liligumma doesn't figure into it."

"Oh, you have disappointed us, Srikant. Is there any way?"

"Then Sachi, you enlist the support of your local MPs who will impress the powers that be."

⁂

13

Like a bolt from the blue came a transfer order for Srikant. He had spent a year in a working post. To gain more experience in other segments, he was being transferred to Chakradharpur Division. Just when he was getting familiar with the surroundings, feeling one with the locals and almost falling in love with its pristine purity, the transfer had struck him, much like lightning.

After bidding goodbye to Sachidanand at Agradoot, Srikant's jeep automatically veered towards Kumud's school. Kumud's heartbreak was palpable.

"When are you leaving?"

"Tomorrow, I will catch the train from Rayagada."

"What time is your train?"

"At 2 p.m."

"When will you come next?" Her voice was choking.

"Can't say. I will write to you."

There was not much scope to talk. Some children gathered round him, "Namaste, Railway Sir!"

"Hello, guys! Remember the picnic? Would you all like to go on a study tour to Puri-Bhubaneswar?"

"Yes, Sir," was their chorus.

After a few minutes of silence full of unspoken words, Srikant left.

The next day, Kumud was at Rayagada station.

"You didn't say you would come," said Srikant.

"Is there freedom for girls to go anywhere as they please? I have come under the excuse that there is some work at the Rayagada subdivision office … when will you come next?"

"I will inform you when I do."

"Will you remember us?"

"Certainly."

One Inspector, a driver and a peon of Srikant's unit had also come to see him off. There was not much scope for Kumud to say anything more.

"This tiffin carrier is for you. Do tell us how you like the besan laddu."

"Why did you take so much trouble?" said Srikant, and suddenly he held her hand. "Arre! Why are your palms so hot?"

"I had a slight fever last night."

"Then why did you come all the way? And how will you return? It will get late. If you don't mind, our jeep will return to Liligumma camp. The driver will drop you. I will tell him."

The signals for his train came off. Srikant got into the compartment. The wheels started to chug. Till it went out of sight, Kumud kept standing on the platform.

"Madam, let us go," the driver called.

14

The Kurla-Howrah express via Jharsuguda reached Chakradharpur station at about 7 a.m. The station, Chakradharpur, reminded Srikant of a trip he had taken during his training. That was two years ago. Platform No. 1 resembled a godown. Everywhere, piles of parcel gunnies were lying around. Cycles were left hither-thither. Rickshawallahs and tangawallahs were crowding at the entrance of the station. Locals were squatting with their wares on the way, and wooden carts were all over the place.

The roof of the station was made of asbestos. It was a sign of the miserliness of the Bengal Nagpur Railway.

At the time of probation, the freshers had commented on the pitiable condition of the station, despite the fact that S.E. Railway earned the maximum revenue.

The officers' guest house was within a distance of one kilometre from the station. As Srikant's arrival was unexpected, no one had come to receive him. Srikant took a rickshaw and reached the guest house. After he introduced himself as the new Assistant Engineer (AEN), the caretaker paid great attention to him. The guest house was under the engineering department after all.

He reported to the Senior Divisional Engineer (Sr DEN), sharp at 10 a.m. Chakradharpur didn't boast of any good schools or colleges, or even a cinema hall; due to this, young officers were reluctant to accept a post there. The Sr. DEN, Dharmapal was happy to get a young engineer. He took Srikant to Divisional Railway Manager (DRM) Mathur Sahib for a courtesy call.

After the preliminary enquiries, came the inevitable question, "Are you married?"

"No, Sir."

"Where have you worked earlier?"

"Waltiar division. In construction."

"You haven't worked in an open-line?"

"No, Sir."

"Do you know the Chakradharpur division is the highest loading division in the Indian Railways?"

"I know, Sir."

"Work is challenging here," the DRM nodded, "After every two stations, you will find one loading siding. Iron ore, limestone, dolomite, manganese—this is a storehouse of all types of minerals. This division has two big steel plants and many cement plants."

He turned back to look at the chart hung behind him.

"Look at the statistics of the division. Every year, we break the loading record," a self-congratulatory smile crossed his face.

"Have tea." The peon had placed the tea tray.

"Where shall we post this young man?" the DRM asked the Sr. DEN.

A phone call interrupted them.

"This is from the Chief Controller (CHC)."

"Where is the derailment?" asked the DRM.

The voice from the other side was loud enough.

"In Badajamda-Nuamundi station. Kilometres 242/12-13."

"How many wagons?"

"Ten, Sir."

"Loaded?"

"Yes, Sir."

"Dharmapal, we all have to go. Get ready. Young man! This derailment has decided your posting. Your posting will be in Dangoapasi. Maximum derailment and rail fractures occur in this section. I will tell the PA to take out your order."

A siren was sounded. Three long ones, in a row.

"Srikant! Bring your luggage to the station. I will also go home to get the line box. Then we will catch the relief train," Dharmapal said.

The relief train came to the platform from the bahrline[1] of the yard. A saloon for the DRM was attached. With the DRM sat the Senior Divisional Engineer (Sr. DEN), Senior Divisional Mechanical Engineer (Sr. DME), Senior Divisional Signal & Telecom Engineer (Sr. DSTE), Senior Divisional Electrical Engineer–Operations (Sr. DEE–OP), Divisional Safety Officer (DSO) and other officials.

Srikant, along with other officers and inspectors, got into the first-class compartment. The gangmen with their shovels, spades and other tools, sat in the BFR wagon.[2] Behind the relief train was attached a crane of one hundred and twenty tonne capacity, because of which their speed could not exceed more than forty kilometres. It took them almost three hours to reach the site.

Before the relief train, Area Superintendent (ARS), and formerly posted AEN, had already reached the site. The wagons that were not damaged had been sent to Badajamada and Dangoapasi station. Only the derailed and capsized wagons were found, which had fallen and blocked two rail lines. The iron ore had fallen on the tracks, and it looked like a mountain.

The afternoon sun was blazing. Emergency light was fixed at the site. Tents were put up. The site phone was installed, and work started on a war footing.

---

1   Entry point to a loco shed
2   Flat type wagon for carrying long products.

Standing at the site, the DRM personally supervised the work. The capsized wagons were pushed down the track with the help of cranes. The remaining wagons were brought back on the rails with the help of cranes and a jack. The re-railing work continued to the wee hours of the morning. Till then, none got a wink of sleep.

The engineering department provided food for everybody. It was cooked in the relief train by the employees. Even after all the senior officers had left, the officers from the engineering department, the SrDEN and two AENs kept working till the tracks were repaired. They had to ensure all-obstacles cleared before a certificate could be given that the tracks could not take a speed beyond ten kilometres.

Finally, when the Sr. DEN's jeep arrived, he offered to drop Srikant off at the guest house. He told the Inspector of Works (IOW) and Permanent Way Inspector (PWI) to take care of Srikant, the new AEN.

For Srikant, it was a memorable first day in his new posting.

15

Dangoapasi had neither vacant quarters nor any other arrangements for Srikant to stay in. He had to make good with one room in the guesthouse. In fact, one type II quarters had been converted to a guesthouse. Each station under Dangoapasi: Badajamada, Barbil, Nuamundi, Gua, Bolanikhadan, Banspanihad one or two railway sidings. From these sidings, the iron ores were mainly carried to the steel plants and exported to Paradeep Port. Rail fractures in these areas was a daily occurrence due to the heavy weight of the wagons. The iron ore dust falling from the wagons used to damage the ballast cushion of the rail tracks and spoil its alignment. This resulted in frequent derailments.

The siren blaring in Dangoapasi yard was a daily occurrence. Srikant soon got used to rushing to the derailment site; sometimes the mainline, sometimes the branch line and at times, in the siding. There were accidents galore in that section. When he was not in the relief train or the saloon, he was found attending the Accident Enquiry Committee.

After a full two weeks, he wrote to Kumud.

"This is my first letter to any girl. Don't know where to start. The place that I am posted is an accident-prone area. I am moving from one accident site to another, like a monkey jumping from one branch to another. The taste of your besan laddu is still fresh in my mouth. Like a miser, I kept saving it, till I finished the last one yesterday.

Did you mind, that day while bidding you goodbye near the train,

I had held your hand in excitement? That feeling is still fresh in my veins. What about you?"

16

Kumud's reply came soon.

"Your letter fell into the hands of my sister. Henceforward please address all letters to my friend Lily Jhodia ..."

Srikant searched for something intimate about the letter. But it was prosaic in the description of her village, her family, and the school. The only redeeming sentence was at the end. *"... Sir, I am embarrassed ... whether to speak of it or not. You have asked whether I felt any excitement when you held my hand. Do you think I am not of age or have crossed the age to experience such excitement?"*

Srikant smiled to himself. The letter was signed with a picture of a lily at the end, while on the top—at the place of an address— was a picture of the moon. The connection between the lily and the moon was symbolic and it filled his heart with a warm flush.

Srikant was at an accident site in Padapahad when a call came to his office at Dangoapasi from Cuttack station. "Sir is at Padapahad station where a derailment has taken place. Please send the message to Padapahad's Station Master," replied his PA.

"Hello, it is a piece of sad news. Srikant Sir's mother passed away today morning. Please convey the message immediately." A porter was sent to the site to convey the message.

Srikant was crestfallen. He wept like a child.

"Sir, I will take you to Dangoapasi in a motor trolley. From there you can go to Tatanagar and catch the Utkal Express."

"No, that will be too late for me to reach my village."

"Then I will tell the contractor to take you to Barabil. From there, you will get a bus or taxi."

"Tell Barbil PWI to book a taxi for me. I have to reach my village tonight somehow. I am the only son."

"Yes, Sir."

The contractor dropped Srikant at Barbil. A taxi was waiting for him.

The road from Barbil to Cuttack was bumpy and treacherous. The loaded trucks with iron ore had wrecked the road. By the time Srikant reached home, it was 1 a.m. in the night. His mother's body was on the pyre, awaiting her final journey. Srikant held her feet and wailed.

17

On return from his village after the funeral, Srikant received news of his promotion as Divisional Engineer (DEN) and his posting back to Chakradharpur Headquarters. Chakradharpur is one of the un-integrated portions of Odisha. About seventy per cent of the population were Odia-speaking. On reaching Chakradharpur, he immersed himself in social work during his spare time. Soon, he became very popular among the Odia-speaking employees; but the loss of his mother had created a vacuum in his life. He had written about his mother's passing to Kumud. Kumud was deeply sympathetic. She wrote back.

"I wish I could come and spend some time with you during your bereavement. But how to go? What can I say at home? Here, everyone is suspicious of me. When will you come again? Can you not take a transfer back? Construction work is going on in full swing here. A big, demon-like machine works full time. The pillars of the bridge look like they are touching the sky. Work of the stations—Sikarpai, Rauli, Tikri, is going on in full speed. The whole day, the hills are reverberating with the sound of dynamite. One small request, can you not make a small station near our village? If not, you come back. You started the work. You should complete it. Do not become like a Viswakarma who made the deities of Srimandir, incomplete in their shape. Koraput is waiting for you."

The people's movement against the alumina factory is becoming stronger and louder. Yesterday, I met your friend, Sachidanand, at the bus stop. He asked me about your whereabouts. He took your address from me."

Srikant kept mulling over her letter. *"Koraput is waiting for you."*

Could it not have been, *"I am waiting for you"*? Why are women so wary of expressing themselves?

18

News came to Srikant that the Baflamali Bauxite mines in Koraput region had been leased by the government to an aluminium company. The local people and the tribals of Koraput were up in arms against mining in their area. The NGOs working in the area raised their voice, while the government was trying to suppress it with all its might. One of the stated objectives of the KR rail line was to facilitate setting up of aluminium industries in the area by tapping into its rich mineral wealth. Srikant thought of writing to his friend Sachidanand of Agradoot NGO that *all* industrialization is not bad, after all. A fine balance between industrialization and protection of ecology is required, without uprooting the tribals and disrupting their way of life.

From Arindam, his ex-boss, he learnt that a tussle was brewing strongly between the state government and the railways with regard to the payment of royalty for mineral ores and cess. After the railways challenged the orders of the state government in the high court, the contractors and rail employees were facing hostility from the state government.

"Srikant! You are experienced in construction organization. Will you like to be posted back to the KR line?" The call came from the CE. Srikant understood, to soften the squabble, the railways have decided to withdraw Odia officers working in other zones and posting them under the KR line.

This was music to Srikant's ears. "Sir, if you order it, I will go," came his polite reply.

He was entitled to ten days joining time, during which he could have gone to his village. But the attraction of Koraput was too strong for Srikant to delay.

19

Srikant's return to his original site came after a gap of a whole year. It was like a homecoming for him. He noticed the number of workers had increased and their camps were teeming and heaving with activity. Some houses had tin roofs, and some were thatched.

Work for the bridges and tunnels were in full swing. So much has progressed, he mused to himself.

One day, the news came that meningitis had spread in the Ganjam slum. Seven persons, including children, had been affected.

Immediately, Srikant called up the Waltiar office. He requested the office send railway doctors. An ambulance was called from Rayagada.

"Sir, why are you so concerned? There are some rules in the railways," Inspector Jagga Rao said.

"Which rule Jagga Rao? Tell me, which rule of Railways are you not breaking?"

"Let us see what the Chief Medical Officer suggests. Before that, we will seek the help of Sachidanand. He is an old-timer in this place. He may have some solution regarding meningitis. Send a jeep to his place."

Srikant then went to Kumud's school and brought her to the site. Sachidanand also arrived, along with some of his people.

In one of the shanties, one person was found sprawling on the floor. He had a vacant look in his eyes and saliva was trickling down his mouth. Among the people surrounding him, one man and one woman looked rather strange. The man, whom people called Disari, was wearing a red turban and was uttering mumbo-jumbo, while holding on to a kusum twig. "Sukru is afflicted by the Goddess," was his refrain. The woman with dishevelled hair and a garland of wildflowers was dancing wildly, in order to drive away the so-called demon from the body of Sukru. His wife was wailing loudly.

"Sukru will not survive," was the chorus. "He is afflicted by the Goddess." They kept repeating the words of the Disari.

"Don't say such nonsense," Kumud almost shouted at the crowd. "This has happened due to the wild mosquitoes. He has to be removed and taken to the hospital immediately. Your mumbo-jumbo is not going to help here."

"Give them Sulpha Diazine tablets. Convince them to keep the surroundings clean and free of mosquitoes," Sachidanand told Kumud.

He had the address of the local doctor. He asked Srikant to send the jeep to fetch him.

Sukru, along with two other labourers, were removed to the local hospital in the contractor's vehicle. Meanwhile, the medical team from Waltiar reached the site.

"Sir, every year a few labourers have been succumbing to meningitis. Thank God, this year they have been removed in time, before it got out of hand. It is all your efforts, Sir." Contractor Harishchandra Baral was appreciative.

"It is not me, but Sachidanand and Kumud who have saved the situation."

20

Srikant was looking for an opportunity to express his thanks to Kumud personally—and privately. What better way, he thought, than to catch her during the school recess? His jeep turned towards the school, but he was told that Kumud was on leave, it being her birthday. Srikant felt a shiver run through him. Sweets and a flower bouquet from Rayagada ... this was his immediate order. In the evening, he made a visit to her house with much trepidation.

"It is your birthday and you haven't told me?"

"Who told you?"

"Your school told me. Here are my birthday wishes for you," and he handed over the bouquet with the sweets and a smile.

"We don't celebrate birthdays. I simply fast and go to the temple."

"But are you still fasting?"

"No."

"Then have the sweets."

"Why did you get so much?"

She called her sister, Pankajini, and handed over the packet. "Get the lantern, Pankaja. Also some tea."

"Only tea will not do," Srikant demanded.

Kumud went inside to make some arrangements and came back to the room. A gust of wind from the outside snuffed out the wick in the lantern. Darkness engulfed the room. Srikant and Kumud sat in comfortable silence, partaking of the darkness.

From inside the house rose a prickly silence. "Pankaja! Get a candle," Kumud shouted from the drawing-room.

"There are no candles at home," came the reply from inside the house.

"Then bring the lantern from the kitchen."

"But our cooking is not over here in the kitchen!"

Kumud got up with the unlit lantern and came back with its wick lit, and placed it in the room. "Please sit for a while," Srikant requested.

After some time, she came back with a plate of hot pooris, curry and kheer in two katoris. She went back inside for a glass of water, when came a voice, "Please tell your guest to wash the plate after taking the food."

"Maa!" screamed Kumud like a person being beaten.

While getting the glass of water, her hands were shivering. Srikant had never seen Kumud in such a disoriented state. He sensed something was awry in the house.

"I can't eat so much. I can only have sweets. I have a weakness for it. Also, I have to return to the camp; rains may break out any time."

Srikant ate the sweet dish and got up. Kumud's eyes were filling with tears. The flickering lantern in the room hid it well.

21

Lightning flashed in the distant hills. The rain God, Indra Dev's, light missiles fell, one after another at Deomali, Baflamali and Sasu Bohumali hills. The parched hills and the earth were waiting with their mouths agape. The trees and plants were craving for a few drops of water.

In the tent, Srikant was discussing his plan of action with his colleagues.

"It is going to rain today. But pre-monsoon rains can be deadly," he exclaimed.

"Yes. Sir, we have to be vigilant. Snakes, crabs and scorpions will come out," indicated Balaram Singh, the Inspector.

"You are talking about snakes and scorpions. I am worried about what will happen to the tunnel," Srikant said. "The fixing of steel strut and ribs have remained incomplete."

He was looking out from the window of the tent. It was getting darker outside. The wind howled like a herd of foxes. The sal trees swayed like dancers possessed. After some time, an old tree fell with a crack. The birds whirled in panic.

"Will the trees fall on the tent?" the employees shuddered. Then lashed the rains, in poured cats and dogs. It showed no signs of stopping.

"The Tunnel No. 23 will not stand. All stay prepared for tomorrow morning," Srikant warned everybody present in the tent.

The incessant rains continued till the next morning. Water had accumulated on the roof of the tunnel and it had caved in, reported the guard. Srikant and his team rushed to the tunnel from Liligumma camp.

With umbrella in hand, Srikant went up the tunnel with an inspector and a gangman.

The khandolite stone floor resembled a bald man's head. Very few shrubs remained; the onslaught of rains had washed away the topsoil. Water had seeped into the crevices and had given way to the tunnel. When he was inspecting the upper floor of the tunnel, the stones and earth in the mouth of the tunnel caved in. The shriek of his workers below rang a bell in his head. He came rushing down. His peon, Hazari, was not in a position to speak.

Srikant grew anxious.

"Had anyone gone inside the tunnel?"

"Yes. Inspector Raghabendra Babu and two gangmen had gone inside."

"Oh shit!" Srikant slumped on the temporary shed in front of the tunnel.

No, he could not be so disconcerted. He had to face this. Some voice in his head cornered him.

"Go to Contractor Harish Babu and tell him to divert all the workers from tunnel no 22 and 24," he told Jagga Rao.

"Meanwhile, the workers of this tunnel must be on their way. I will make them clear the mounds of earth. Tell Harish Babu to bring the emergency phone and the emergency light. And don't spread the news that workers are trapped inside the tunnel. If the local people, or the press and police get to know, they will not let us work. Tell him to get lots of foodstuffs, like rice and dal, vegetables, banana, bread—whatever else."

He then went up the tunnel and tried to contact Raghabendra Rao, but only his voice echoed back to him.

With the emergency phone, he tried to contact Kolkata Headquarters and the bosses at Vishakhapatnam. He called for the ambulance from Rayagada. Workers from three sites were at work on a war footing. Food was being cooked for all who were present there.

By evening, the mouth of the tunnel had been cleared. Then started the search for Raghabendra Rao and his two gangmen.

With searchlights on, the three of them were found safe, huddled in a stony hole. They were so traumatized that they could hardly speak.

They were given food to eat and were sent back to the camp to rest.

Raghabendra Rao lifted up his hands and exclaimed, *"Tirupati Baba ki jay ho!"*

The clearing of the tunnel went on under the emergency lights.

❖ ❖ ❖

22

Next day, the CE from Kolkata and the CE (Con) from Waltiar descended on the site. Also came, the Dy CE (Con), Arindam Ghosh. All of them visited the accident site and then sat in the camp, huddled for a meeting.

"The holes in the stone floor can be closed with a concrete canopy. But that procedure is expensive. The other alternative is jet grouting."

"Sir we can use this alternative here. Konkan railways have used this procedure," Srikant interrupted.

The CE (Con) supported Srikant's proposal.

"Our resources are limited. So we will go for grouting. Along with it, we have to do enough drainage on the upper portion of the hill so that the water will not accumulate."

Both the chief engineers returned in the evening, while Arindam Ghosh and Srikant stayed back at the site.

The evening of the next day, the cleaning of the tunnel was completed. The rains had stopped. While having tea, Arindam and Srikant were chalking out the plan for obtaining the grouting machine from Bangalore. The contractor had asked for seven days. Dharamu, the tribal coolie sardar along with his workers, came to meet them.

"What happened Dharamu?"

"Sahib, we want to say something …"

"Okay, go on."

"Sahib. Dharani Penu is angry here. If we don't placate her, she will break the tunnel again and again. This was the second time. Three times means that it is dangerous. This time, two people were saved by the breadth of a hair. After this, no one will survive."

Both Arindam and Srikant broke into uproarious laughter.

Dharamu's face fell.

The Telugu Inspector, Jagga Rao, sitting nearby commented, "Sir, I think Dharamu has come here after a drink of salap."

"Don't infuriate Dharani Penu further by such talk, Inspector Garu," admonished Dharamu.

"Okay, why don't you tell us what will make Dharani Penu happy?"

"Sir, here you have to sacrifice a goat."

"You want a feast, is that why you are asking for this?"

"You, Telenga Babu, are not listening; you will pay the price."

Srikant intervened, "Sir, if the workers want it, let us have a puja here. Adivasis have a custom of animal sacrifice for their worship. Let it be a hen, a fowl or a goat."

"Okay, let it be so. You all have mutton. You know what I want with mutton," smiled Arindam.

"Take the money, get a goat, and you will have a feast at night. Tell your friends to finish their work fast," Srikant said to them.

Dharamu and his friend hopped away in glee. With the goat came Jani and Disari. Jani made the sacrifice, collected the blood of the goat in a leaf chalice and gave it as an offering near the mouth of the tunnel, all the while mouthing "abracadabra".

The feast was accompanied by the sound of changu and madal. Salap flowed like the river. Arindam sat with his drink, while Srikant shook a leg with the revellers.

❖ ❖ ❖

23

Nilamani, Kumud's brother, came home on a holiday after a long period of waiting. Nilamani was the Habildar of the Bihar Regiment. His mother and sisters were overjoyed to see him. His new posting was to be in Ladakh. His father had also finished his duties at the mandir and had come home early.

While having lunch, all the family members kept pestering him to share his life experiences in the army—its food, its way of life.

But Nilamani was grave. He popped up, "Maa, while getting down at the bus stop, I saw Kumud going in a jeep with another person. Who is this person?"

Pankajini and Kallolini shared meaningful glances.

"Beta, he is a railway engineer. Some epidemic has broken out in the railway shanties; Kumud has gone with him to help the people."

"How is he?"

"Seems to be a good boy. He has come home—once or twice. Why do you ask?"

"I have seen a boy for Kumud. He is posted in our regiment; very fair and handsome chap. He is from Jajpur. A brahmin of Atreya gotra. He will rise quickly in the army and become an officer soon."

"Okay, let Kumud come. We will finalize after talking with her."

Kumud returned late in the evening, she was overjoyed to see her brother. She heard from her sisters about her brother's proposal. It was as if a bomb had exploded on her.

Nilamani was not exactly happy to see her.

"Coming late from school, is it?"

"No, today is a holiday."

"Who were you going with in a jeep this morning?"

"His name is Srikant Das. You must have seen the rail line work going on. He is in charge of the project."

"I know. How is he as a person?"

"Good person."

"I have found out from his camp that he belongs to a lower caste."

Kumud was speechless.

"It may be so. I have never been bothered about it."

"I have selected a boy for you."

"Bhai, I will take care of myself. I cannot marry an army guy."

"Why?"

"What will happen to my job here?"

"Do you imagine that you will marry that railway engineer?"

Kumud did not reply.

"Dreaming about roaming from Kashmir to Kanyakumari, are you? Becoming a sahibani?"

Kumud still did not reply.

Her father returned after conducting the evening prayers.

Supporting Nilamani, he said, "Have you thought about what

will happen to us? We are high caste Brahmins. Barsiban gotra. If you take any such step what will happen to your two younger sisters? Who would like to have any relations with us? Our caste people will spurn us."

Tears flowed from Kumud's eyes.

"If you do anything like that, I will kill and hang you from the nearest tree."

No one present said a word in support of Kumud. She dragged herself to her bedroom and dropped down on the bed.

This is the brother on whom she ties a rakhi every year, and extracts a promise that he will keep her safe? This is the brother for whom she does Khudurukuni Brata and prays before Devi Mangala for his well-being? It is the end of twentieth century, but people have still not overcome the barriers of caste! What is the point in being educated and self-reliant when one doesn't have the freedom to decide one's own destiny? Kumud felt that she was suffocating in this patriarchal household.

24

It was around midnight. Srikant was perusing his files; his staff had retired for the day, when he heard footsteps near his tent. He got up from his sofa.

"Who is there?"

There was no response.

But like a wave gushing towards the shore, Kumud entered the tent. A gale. She almost fell on him. Her breathing was heavy, and she was trembling. Srikant held her in his arms.

"So late in the night and alone?"

Kumud was not able to speak.

"Tell me Kumud, what is the matter?"

"Sir, please rescue me. My brother has come. He is creating a ruckus at home after seeing us together … He has fixed a boy for me and wants to marry me off. Please … save me."

Srikant slowly released her from his arms and made her sit on the sofa; he then poured water from the jug into a tumbler and made her drink it.

Her footwear was dishevelled, and the edge of her sari was wet to the ankles, probably because she had waded through the muddy waters to reach his tent.

"Kumud, let us wait with patience for the opportune time.

We cannot take any step hoodwinking society, government and the police."

"Sir, please do something. You can do it. Let us go away from this place for some time. Time will solve everything."

Srikant was rendered speechless. He was not able to determine what he should do.

"Please … leave me in your village or some other safe place."

"See, I have no one in my village, you know that Kumud. Besides, how can I leave the responsibility of this camp to anyone without permission from my boss?"

He held Kumud's hand and pleaded, "Let us not wake up the staff with our talk, please. Have trust in me, Kumud. I will wait for you."

"Sir … I …" her words, which must have come from the depths of her soul, were somehow not able to reach her trembling lips.

In that pregnant silence, she looked at Srikant and got up. Foxes were howling in these wee hours. An owl hooted away. It was pitch black outside the tent. In that dense darkness, Srikant drove up the road, right up to the outskirts of her village.

"Please stop here. If my brother sees us, he will create a scene. I will walk."

The headlight of the jeep illuminated the road for Kumud to walk back home. She looked back frequently. Her feet were moving ahead, but her mind kept turning her around. Or was she wondering when she would meet Srikant again?

25

The next morning Srikant got up late, feeling languorous. Last night's sudden events had left him in a stupor. He was not in a mood to go to the site. Scene by scene, the events of the previous night kept replaying in his mind.

Why couldn't he take things into his hand? Why was he unsure, irresolute? In that dark night, rising above the inclement weather and fear of wild animals, Kumud had come running to him, leaving behind the security and comfort of her parents' home, away from those who had lovingly raised her. In a bold stroke, she had scaled the wall of her high caste standing in society and come to a man who was in the pale of the so-called caste pecking-order. She was clearly in love, and love is blind. Perhaps she hoped, that Srikant, like a prince in shining armour, would rescue her; she the damsel in distress.

But why couldn't he muster up enough courage to accept her then and there? What was lacking in him as a man? Is the middle class not entitled to love like the higher class aristocrats and the lower class workers?

Lembua interrupted his thoughts.

"Sir, a madam has come to meet you."

Srikant got up in a flurry, thinking it might be Kumud again. But it was Lily Jhodia, Kumud's colleague and friend.

"Sir, Kumud's family came to know of her visit to you in the middle of the night yesterday. They are burning with rage. Her brother and father's fury were directed towards both of you. Her father was lamenting that he would rather die before his Brahmin daughter marries the fisherman's son. It is the opposite of what happened in the Mahabharat, where a fisherman's daughter married the sage, Parashar. He wailed so much that it led to a heart attack. He has been removed to Rayagada hospital. Kumud has gone with him. All these things she conveyed to me through a small chit."

She continued. "Kumud is in danger. Sir, please do something."

Srikant sat down, stupefied.

Lily left in a huff.

26

The GM Special, carrying officers from Kolkata Headquarters with the purpose of inspecting the new railway line, reached Rayagada station before 6 a.m. Much before its arrival, a commotion had spread through the station.

A special train carrying the officials of the division had reached the night before. These officials were ready and pacing up and down the platform to receive the GM. Officers, inspectors, substaff … together numbering about a hundred, had gathered in the platform. Some had flower bouquets in their hands, some had maps and time-tables and the railway rule book in their hands.

As per schedule, breakfast would be over by 8 a.m., after which would start the inspection. The CE (Con), the DRM, and the others were waiting in front of the saloon.

The door of the saloon opened. At the door appeared a person of five and a half feet height, with two-thirds of his hair no longer on his head, attired in jeans and a half shirt. He looked quite nondescript, but he received a welcome apt for a king.

He waved to the gathering. The saloon attendant cleaned the door handle, after which he got down. The first to welcome him with flower bouquet was the Station Master. Then came the DRM and the secretaries of the two unions. The photographers assigned by the division and the headquarters did their job. After the welcoming formalities were over, he went to the observation car. The observation car had a window trailing. A big table was placed near the window, along with three seats. The GM sat on the chair at the centre, while the DRM and CE sat on two sides, opposite him. Behind him were rows of chairs. Other divisional heads and officers occupied the chairs behind them.

The CE placed the map on the table and gave a brief account of the KR line. He reiterated that the KR line has thirty-six tunnels, sixty-seven big bridges, three hundred and sixty-nine small bridges and twelve stations.

As per the programme, the first halt was near Tunnel No. 23.

"Sir, you must have heard about this tunnel. This tunnel crashed twice. Only due to this tunnel, our work was delayed by three months," said the CE.

"I know. I hope there is no danger now."

"No, Sir. It has been set right by working day and night."

"Who is in charge of this section?"

"Srikant Das."

"Please note," the GM ordered his Secretary. "Award of fifty thousand rupees for the DEN and his team. Who is this Srikant Das?"

Srikant moved up ahead and introduced himself.

"Thank you, Sir."

"Are there provisions for ventilation in this tunnel?"

"Yes, Sir."

The train stayed in the tunnel for a while and then moved ahead. Then came Bridge no. 130. It was built on the river Jhanjabati.

"This bridge is the longest and highest," the CE (Con) commented.

Down below the bridge lay the thin river; on both its sides stood thickest of jungles. "Wonderful," the GM commented after surveying the place.

Tea and snacks were served.

Not very far from the inspection train, a crowd of locals were waiting for the GM Special. They had red flags in their hands. They were mouthing slogans.

"*Inquilab Zindabad!*"

The throng included lots of tribal men and women. The banner was held by two persons standing in the middle of the railway track. The legend, "Liligumma Sangharsh Samiti" could be seen.

From Tunnel No. 23, a long whistle, like the trumpet of an elephant, was sounded. Now, other people jumped on to the track. The slogans became louder.

"GM, go back!"

"*Inquilab Zindabad!*"

The gangman blowing his whistle as he stood near the entrance of the tunnel with a red flag was communicating to the driver through signs. The driver reduced the speed of the train. After the train slowly slithered out of the tunnel, the crowd of agitators could finally be seen. Srikant was mildly surprised to see the agitation being led by his friend, Sachidanand.

The Sr. DME was on the footplate. He had the V.H.F set with him. He messaged the Sr. DOM.

"Sir, there is a rail roko ahead."

"What is the reason?" asked the GM.

"Let me find out." The Security Commandant got down from the observation car. Seeing him, the Railway Protection Force (RPF) Inspector and his armed guard got down from the brake van.

On seeing the railway personnel getting down from the train, the agitators' voices grew louder.

The Commandant went near them. "What is the reason for this rail roko?"

Sachidanand came in front. He asked his people to stay quiet.

"The local people want a station in this place."

Commandant halted his armed forces near the crowd and came back to the observation car. "Sir, they want a station to be built here."

The Inspector General (IG RPF) was sitting near the GM. "If you order it, I will disperse the crowd with blank fire," said the IG (RPF).

"No, there is no need to create such an unpleasant situation. Call their leader. Let us hear him out."

Commandant went to the agitators and spoke to Sachidanand.

"The GM has called you for a meeting. Come to the train."

"No, no. Call your GM here. Let him speak his promises before this crowd. Only then will they disperse."

Meanwhile, Srikant had got down from the train and reached the gathering. He whispered something into Sachidanand's ear. Sachidanand agreed to go to the train, and twenty people followed him.

"So many people cannot go in. Only two or three can go," requested the Commandant.

On Srikant's gesture, Sachidanand agreed. One woman and one man accompanied Sachidanand.

The Secretary was standing at the gate of the observation car.

"Come up and have a cup of tea with us," he said.

Sachidanand and his friends climbed the observation car. Some twenty officers focused on him. The Secretary introduced the GM and his officers to Sachidanand.

"I am Sachidanand. I have an NGO here. I work for the local people here."

"What is your demand?" asked the GM.

"This place is an important site in the Koraput-Rayagada rail line. You have made stations for the obscure places. The nearest station is ten kilometres away from this place. It is not possible to walk to the place in such hilly terrain. What benefit of the rail line is reaped by these people?"

"See, you cannot make stations at every site. The Railway Board has taken into consideration the location of the place, the distance between stations, the budget of the project and other things, after which they have decided accordingly. It is not in my hands."

"See, I have not come in to have tea. You promise our people that you will make a station here. Without that promise, they will not move." The two persons who had accompanied Sachidanand repeated the demand.

Sachidanand asked his comrades to keep quiet.

"Sir, you are all from the Railways. If you want, you can do everything. If a Divisional Superintendent is giving the order to make a new station, why can't you do it?"

"Which Divisional Superintendent you are talking about?"

"About Khurda Road division. It was during my childhood. My house was in a small village, in Puri district. We used to see the people travelling by the Puri-Howrah line every day. To go to Puri or Cuttack, we had to go via Jatni or Delang to catch the trains of that line. We used to travel by a bullock cart to get there; and in the rainy seasons, it was difficult. But this problem was solved by the DS."

"How?"

"The DS's wife had an illness. No allopathy, homoeopathy or ayurvedic medicine could cure her. Someone suggested the name of a doctor in our village to him. The doctor examined his wife and suggested that she stop all medication and asked her to follow some diet. Within two months, she was completely cured. The DS was so grateful to the doctor that he asked if he wanted anything in return for his services. The doctor said he would not take a pie. Instead, he asked if the DS could do him a favour, by making a railway station in his village. The DS said it would be done."

The next day, railway engineers came to our village, surveyed and measured the place. Soon, the gangmen came with their tools, and a place in our village was cleared. Within a few days, the bushes were cleared, and a platform stood in its place; within a month there was a station, booking office, waiting room etc."

"Oh, then a passenger halt was constructed," remarked GM.

"Yes Sir, if the DS could do it, you are much above him. Why can't you do it?"

The GM looked at the CE and the CCM. "Sir, DRMs do not have that power now. But we can tell him to verify the site and send a proposal to us, which can be forwarded to the Railway Board 'said CCM."

"Okay, I will get the place surveyed and send the proposal to the Board. You have to wait for some time."

"No, you have to declare in front of our people that a passenger halt will be made, otherwise they will not move from here."

The rail roko had gone on for an hour. The GM was getting restless. He looked at the CCM.

"Sir, you have within your delegated powers to make a small halt where the annual loss is within rupees ten thousand. If the loss goes beyond that number, the case will go to Railway Board."

"Tell your people to travel by train and to buy tickets," the GM told Sachidanand.

"You don't worry about that. But afterwards, you make it a regular halt."

"Okay. Now tell your people to lift the rail roko. We are hungry."

Sachidanand looked at Srikant. A smile crossed his face and he got down from the observation train.

27

The rail line work was coming to an end. After the tracks and bridges, a few constructions on the station building remained. The camp at Liligumma was to be wound up.

Srikant was throwing a dinner for the workers. He had told contractor Baral to pay them their pending dues. On that wintry December night, the workers had made a bonfire and were sitting huddled around it. Someone threw a dry log. The fire crackled greedily, chewing on it. The hard faces of the workers looked auburn against the leaping flames. Some of the workers were quietly smoking their bidis, while some were chattering away. Smatterings of their conversation filtered through the window of the tent.

"I will have to give my daughter in marriage after returning. I wonder where I will get all the money for gold, silver, utensils, clothes, everything? I will have to again stretch my palms before the sahukar," one worker was lamenting.

"I will have to release my wife's ornaments from the moneylender," another one added.

"Where will be our next destination?" some speculated.

One young Chhattisgarhi worker was being prodded to sing a song. The voice of the young man was mellifluous, but the song was full of pathos; it spoke of some old wound, perhaps of separation from a loved one. Srikant, sitting near the window of the tent, was reminded of Shelly's immortal lines, "Our sweetest songs are those that tell of our saddest thoughts."

One worker from Ganjam broke into a song, "*Thakamana chala jiba! Chaka Nayan dekhiba. Sankha nabhi mandalare beni netra pakhaliba.* (O tired mind! Let us visit Jaganath Dham. On seeing the round-eyed God, our eyes will be purified.)" Another joined him, playing the cymbals and the khanjani. Both were drenched in their devotion for Lord Jagannath.

The boisterous feast over, all the workers dropped into a deep slumber. But sleep eluded Srikant's eyes. Kumud's memories were pecking at his heart, like a woodpecker pecking on wood. There was no escape from thoughts of her. It followed him wherever he went. While walking along the rail lines, while winding up office work, while trying to catch a few winks, her face was like a moving image on his mindscape.

✥ ✥ ✥

28

30 December 1995. The KR line will be dedicated to the nation.

The day the news came from the Prime Minister's Office, a ripple spread across the Railway headquarters, Waltiar division, the state capital and the construction organization.

The work of Koraput-Rayagada line had been completed. Employees had been posted at the new stations.

However, finishing-touches for the Liligumma passenger halt remained. Srikant saw to it that it was completed before D-day. He had already inaugurated the station with the help of the village chiefs and his friend, Sachidanand, Director of NGO Agradoot.

Preparations were afoot for the Prime Minister's inauguration at the Kolkata office. All the departmental heads, the CE, DRM/Waltiar and other high ranking officials participated. It was decided that:

- PM will land in Rayagada by helicopter. From there, his cavalcade will travel by road to the police ground, which had been fixed as the venue.

- The CE will prepare a blueprint of the podium.

- The CPRO will prepare a draft of the advertisements, invitation cards, pamphlets and put them up to the GM.

- A sketch will be made of the seating arrangements of the VIPs, press representatives and the public, and submitted for the approval of the SPG.

- A guest list of those who will be seated on the podium will be prepared and sent to the PMO.

- After the meeting, tea and refreshments will be served to the guests; the CCM will take the responsibility.

- While travelling from Rayagada helipad to the meeting ground, a level-crossing check gate has to be crossed. The DRM has to ensure that the level-crossing gate remains open at that time.

- For compeering the show, an attractive lady with an attractive voice has to be engaged; the CPRO will ensure it.

- From the headquarters, the GM, CE, CME, CCM, COM, CSTE, IG (RPF), FA & CAO will travel to Rayagada by a special train and reach Rayagada a day before.

- The Construction organization will construct the podium and the meeting enclosure.

- The CPRO will bring the press team from Kolkata and reach early in the morning.

- Full-page advertisements will be made on the previous, and the same day, on all the national and regional dailies.

- The IG (RPF) will coordinate with the SPG to ensure security and maintain law and order.

- The DRM will take care to send invitation cards to all local MPs, MLA, Zonal Railway Users' Consultative Committee (ZRUCC) and Divisional Railway Users' Consultative Committee (DRUCC).

29

The bandobast at the Police ground was impressive. The shamiana was meant for about five thousand people. But the stage was meant for five VIPs only—the PM, the CM, Rail Minister, Governor and Chief Secretary of the Odisha government. The rest of the chairs had been removed. The GM didn't have a chair earmarked for him; rather, he was asked to conduct the proceedings while standing at the podium, thus making the cine star's services redundant. Coming all the way from Bhubaneswar, she felt slighted, but the fees were paid to her anyway. Some press people were handed passes at the last minute, after much protest.

On landing at Rayagada helipad, the PM was greeted by the five VIPs, but the Railway Senior Officers were not allowed to offer bouquets.

By the time the PM's convoy started from Rayagada helipad, the Vishakhapatnam-Titlagarh Passenger had left Rayagada station. It was expected that within two minutes it would cross the level-crossing gate. But the chain had been pulled by some miscreant, which resulted in the train halting at the level-crossing gate. The SP on duty screamed that he would arrest the rail officers for not minding his instructions. The Sr. DOM told the Sr. DME, "Just get into the engine. We will tell the driver to create vacuum and pull the train ahead."

"But that will be against safety regulations."

"Forget regulations ... we have to survive first."

"I am getting into the engine, you follow me."

The driver, on his orders, released the brake and took the train ahead at full speed. It crossed the level-crossing with a rumble. The railway officers heaved a sigh of relief.

The convoy reached the venue and the PM pressed the button to dedicate the rail line to the nation. One decorated goods train was kept at the station. It was the first train to drive the section.

The PM's speech continued for fifty minutes. He outlined the schemes meant for the tribal population. "The central government is committed to the development of the tribal-dominated state," was his grand promise.

Srikant was moving across the meeting ground among the public. The speeches of the PM and the Ministers simply went above his head. His ears were in no mood to listen. His eyes were desperately looking for someone. Would magic occur? Will Kumud be seen in this place? But she was not seen that day, nor was she seen after.

30

A few days after the inauguration of KR line came the news—a vigilance case had been slapped against Srikant. Everyone knew that he was a popular and capable engineer. He had been appreciated by the GM for his work when the tunnels were to be restored. After the rail-line work was completed, he was one among the group awardees that had received cash prize of one lakh rupees from the Rail Minister.

Perhaps he was a victim of jealousy among his peers, or it was the result of some written or anonymous complaint. The queries raised by Vigilance included the estimated and actual expenditure of Liligumma station, the details of store material under his supervision, approval from higher-ups for making a halt at Liligumma, approval for selection of spot by the higher-ups and so on.

Srikant replied to the queries with all the details he could find. He met with the CE and apprised him of the vigilance case. But the CE expressed his inability to interfere with vigilance cases, as his promotion to a GM post was due.

His immediate boss, Arindam Ghosh, explained that no senior will have the courage to bail out a junior from a vigilance case.

After a month, he received a memorandum, which stated that he had violated the Railway Service Conduct Rules, 1968. The charges against him were that while selecting the spot of the railway halt, he had not taken prior approval from higher-ups. If the halt had been made at a lower altitude, the cost would have been lower.

Secondly, he had spent beyond the estimated cost.

Thirdly, the labour of the local people in building the station was nominal. He had utilized railway material recklessly.

Fourthly, the approval of the state government is required for naming the station halt. He had done it according to his whims.

Fifthly, instead of inviting the local MPs and MLAs for inaugurating the station, the honours were done by one of his friends.

Srikant consulted his friend, Sachidanand. Sachidanand was apologetic for having demanded the railway stop, for which Srikant was now in a soup. Srikant, however, assured him that it was the work of some jealous colleague or another. Sachidanand promised that he would meet Srikant's GM and take the help of the local MP to rescue him from such a predicament.

Srikant said, "You know, Sachi, during the first World War, in Soviet Russia, one commissar had increased the speed of the trains carrying the soldiers and war equipment to facilitate speedy delivery. In return, the Soviet government hanged him to death; on the grounds that he caused more wear and tear of the tracks by using the fast-moving trains, thereby hampering the wartime safety of the country. This government has only charge-sheeted me. This may take away my job, but not my life anyway."

"Oh my God! You are joking even in such trying times? What if you lose your job? What will you do?"

"You will give me a job."

Both the friends broke into laughter.

"You are always welcome, Srikant."

31

A retired FA&CAO, by the name B.K. Mitra was appointed as an Enquiry Officer for conducting an enquiry into the vigilance case. The date and venue of the enquiry were communicated to Srikant. Mr Mitra was an easy-going Bengali officer without much of an ego.

From the Vigilance side, the presenting officer was deputed from the Railway Board. As per the rules to help Srikant, a defence counsel could have been appointed. His ex-boss, Arindam Ghosh, volunteered to assist as the defence counsel. But Srikant did not agree and informed inwriting that he will fight his own case. In the first session, he pleaded not guilty to all the accusations levelled at him.

The next sitting was held at Rayagada. It was the headquarters of the Dy CE (Con) and housed most of the documents of the KR line.

On the appointed day, witnesses from both sides were present. Srikant started his defence.

Firstly, the approval for the passenger halt at Liligumma had been received. So he had not violated any official rules.

Secondly, Srikant was delegated the task of selecting the spot for the railway halt. The place mentioned in the charges had a big slope on both sides with high curvature. So he had selected an alternative site.

Thirdly, the expenditure for the halt did not exceed the estimate. The local people not only gave free labour but also supplied material, which gave the impression that more than the estimate was spent. He submitted a copy of the list of construction material received from the NGO Agradoot to the enquiry.

Fourthly, the naming of the station was done after the nearest village. A letter, seeking the approval of the State government was sent. But no reply was received from the State. One could have always sought post-facto approval.

Fifthly, the inauguration of the halt station had to be completed before the inauguration of the KR line by the Prime Minister. There was hardly any time left for inviting any of the MPs, or MLAs, within such a short period.

Presenting Officer and his witnesses could not provide any strong evidence in support of their argument.

The Enquiry Officer proposed that he would visit the disputed site himself. The next day, he started in the motor trolley for Liligumma. His employees and other officers went in a jeep. The night's stay was arranged at the Laxmipur Railway Guest House.

Mr Mitra was a poet at heart. He was enchanted by the dense sal piasal forest on both sides of the track. On seeing the station atop the hill, he commented, "Srikant, you have constructed a mini-Taj Mahal."

"Sir, you have seen the stations under the South Eastern Railway. They look so deplorable. In contrast, the stations under the Western Railway and Southern Railway are so fine. The income of South Eastern Railway is more than theirs. But there is such a miserly attitude while constructing the stations and providing facilities for passengers. I have made arrangements for all kinds of passenger facilities, in fact, more than is required, keeping in mind its future expansion into a full-fledged station."

"Your arguments are right. But the facilities provided should have been as per the norms, which is based on a passenger survey."

"Sir, the norms fixed are completely outdated. In the norms, it is mentioned that shade-giving trees should be planted instead of a passenger shed. Isn't that ridiculous? If a halt is made, then isn't a urinal or toilet the basic requirement? How can the norms be silent

about it? You must have read the story of passenger, Okhil Chandra Sen. He had eaten jackfruit and felt the urgency of nature's call. The guard of the train in which he was travelling did not stop the train at Sahibganj station, due to which he was in acute distress, holding on to his tumbler and dhoti. His complaint led to the construction of toilets in the trains. The letter is in display in Delhi Rail museum, Sir."

"I am aware of the incident."

"Sir, I have made passenger facilities forecasting the need for the coming two decades."

Lunch was arranged at Liligumma. After lunch, it was time for a visit to Laxmipur.

"Wonderful. The half-circular platform lies under the canopy of the sal forest like a sleepy damsel in her dreams. It is indeed impressive," commented the Enquiry Officer.

"Sir, this section was not under my command. But we had decided in the first place to make all the stations under the KR line beautiful and comfortable."

In the night, on behalf of the AEN, a dinner party was arranged for the Enquiry Officer. Everyone knew about the tastes of this retired senior officer. So, items of his choice, like mutton kasa, fish curry, egg cutlet, among others were served along with hard drinks. The party went on late into the night.

"See Srikant, I agree with your arguments. I will give a favourable report. But I know of the Board Vigilance. The Board may reject my report. There are many such examples. So you may be punished. But tell me, what will you do if there is a danger to your job?"

"Sir, I have no one behind me. I lost my father when I was a child. I lost my mother recently. I am not married. If nothing, I will stay in this undeveloped tribal area and work for them. I can give vocational training to the tribal kids and help them progress in life."

"I am feeling sleepy Mr Srikant. Before I go to sleep, one last question. Of course, I will not mention this anywhere. But why did you build such an impressive station in the name of a passenger halt and invite problems for yourself?"

"Sir, you are like my father and just as respectable. I will not lie to you. My beloved's village is behind the station, downhill." Mr Mitra became speechless and a faint smile crossed his lips as he fell asleep.

32

"I am back Sachi … and … forever!" shouted Srikant from within a vehicle.

Sachidanand could not believe his eyes. Srikant was getting down from a jeep with a bag and baggage. He got up from his chair, moved to the door and was looking for the right words to say, when Srikant announced, "It has come. Removal from service."

"What?"

"Yes, a memorandum from the railways ... You don't believe me? Shall I show you?"

"No, I don't believe it."

"Yes, my friend, it is a fact."

"But you must be given a chance to appeal?"

"Yes, technically I can, but I won't."

"You can go to court."

"I will not knock at the doors of the court."

"Why not?"

"I don't wish to return to the railways."

"Tell me, your bosses were happy with your work. And you told me that your GM gave you an award. Did you not approach them?

What is the stand of your CE?"

"The CE told me that he cannot interfere with a vigilance case, that is the tradition of the railways. Also, why would he go out of his way to help me? What have I done for him except for working sincerely? I have neither given him any valuable gift nor an air ticket. Rather, he charged me that I did not look after the media, for which the railways got a negative press during the inauguration of the KR line. For what will he canvass my case with the GM?"

He would have continued with his abuses, but the attendant came with cups of tea.

"Good, Srikant, you are here. I am going to Japan for a few weeks. You can look after Agradoot in my absence."

"Why Japan?"

"You remember the book—*One straw Revolution* by Fukuwaka, which I gave you during your last visit here? I am going to his farm to get first-hand experience of his farming techniques, after which I will implement them here in Agradoot."

"Oh, that's nice. You don't worry. I will act as a guardian of Agradoot in your absence."

"But why don't you also come along with me to Japan. The bill will be footed by the farm."

"No, I don't want to go anywhere. I need to go to my village to complete what has been unfinished."

That night, the two friends slept on the roof, under the canopy of the stars. The stars were shining like diamonds and precious jewels upon a clear sky. Srikant was watching the glittering sky, which he had missed all this while, working twenty-four-seven for the railways.

Suddenly Sachi popped up, "Will you not have a family Srikant?"

"But you need a wife to make a family."

"But you must have gotten umpteen proposals as you are in the railway services."

"Yes, they came, but the person I wanted did not come."

"What happened?"

"Society did not approve of our relationship."

"But you could have broken the norms, anyway, you were a hurdle-runner at university."

"One can jump hurdles for oneself and break one's bones. But if you do it for someone else, her life may be in danger."

"Are you talking about Kumudini Madam?"

"Yes."

"See, I had an inkling that you were in love."

A smile crossed Srikant's face. "But how did you guess? You may have seen us only once or twice."

"Someone had said, both, coughing and loving cannot remain hidden."

"Well, where is she now?"

"Can't say. The last I heard, the entire family was taken away to Jammu by her brother in the Army. Her father expired after his heart attack. After that, I have no news from her friend, Lilli Jhodia, because she herself succumbed to malaria. Their house in Liligumma has a big lock hanging on it."

"But you must search for her. Don't give up so easily."

"Tell me, if she has been given in marriage, will it be proper for me to enter her new life?"

33

Fifteen years later ...

Liligumma halt had become a full-fledged station. The KR line had opened up Koraput to the world outside. Tourists thronged to see the forest-wrapped, undulating mountains; the waterfalls, valleys and meadows. Poets wrote about its pristine beauty, writers wrote stories and novels, researchers produced theses on sixty types of tribals, the original inhabitants of the place.

After Koraput was linked to Kolkata, it became an exotic destination for the discerning Bengali tourists. That puja vacation, Fort William Central School Class XI students, along with their two teachers, headed towards Koraput for their holidays.

After Rayagada station passed, the students crowded near the windows. The train was whistling and passing through tunnel after tunnel. Each time it entered the cavern-like pit, a collective sound arose. For the children, it was a magical feeling, as if they were being transported to the world of Harry Potter.

Ira was holding a time-table and watching through the window as station after station passed by. Bhalumaska station was nearing; on both sides were mango orchards.

"Why such a name Madam?" She knew Teacher Madam hailed from Odisha.

"Probably bears were invading the mango orchards."

After Sikarpai, it was a carpet of alasi flowers on both sides of the track. As if the tress had worn a yellow sari, shining bright under the sunlight.

Then came the sal forest. Dense and deep. Liligumma station was approaching. Ira got up from her seat and shouted, "Robin pull the chain, let us see the station."

"But what is there in this particular station?"

"Pull it, na ... I will tell you."

Robin and another student hung on to the chain. With a loud screech like that of a wild elephant, the train came to a grinding halt.

"Why did you stop the train?" Teacher Sir was shouting while the boys and girls got down on the platform and quickly climbed up the steps to the station.

"My grandfather said this station was built by an engineer for his beloved. But he lost his job for making such a beautiful station," Ira told her friends.

Howrah-Koraput Express did not have a stop at Liligumma. The two small and one long whistle irritated the Station Master, the indication for a chain being pulled. "Go, Saraju, see in which bogie the chain has been pulled."

Instead of giving a report for the Howrah-Koraput Express, he was informing the control room "Rao Garu chain pulling."

The middle-aged Station Master of Liligumma, the king of the small station with the sole responsibility of looking after both, operating and commercial section, was talking to his control room, when Ira entered his cabin, "Uncle."

"Yes," he turned away from the phone receiver.

"I wanted to ask one question. Can you tell us which engineer constructed this station and where he stays?"

"How would I know? Is it written anywhere? Why are you asking?"

It was a strange question. He only knew about the present and was totally ignorant of the past.

"My grandfather said that for making such a beautiful station on the hill, the engineer lost his job. Also, he told me that he built it in memory of his beloved."

Now the Station Master put down his receiver and broke into hearty laughter. He spat out the rest of his betel juice into the waste bin and shook his head vigorously.

"Love in the railways? One more Shahjahan in the twenty-first century?"

He laughed. "See, young lady, there is no time in the railways, even to die. Now there's an accident, now a rail roko, sometimes a rail fracture or hot axle in the bogies. If nothing, there are marauding elephants, sliding boulders—you name a problem, it exists in the railways. Even grass doesn't grow under the tracks. How can love grow? Even if someone in the railways harbours it, it gets crushed under the iron wheels of the locomotive. By the way, who is your grandfather?"

"My grandfather B.K. Mitra was Chief Finance Officer of the railways. He is no more." Her voice quivered.

Oh! The Station Master appeared moved, "Go child go, the train will leave now." He spoke like a guardian. In a high-pitched voice, he added, "Children, don't pull the chain. Remember, it is an offence." The long whistle was heard, after which the guard had set the alarm chain right.

The children ran back to the compartment; their teacher was grumbling. "I will report against you people, if you behave like this."

The lady teacher, however, sat unmoving and looked out of the window at the station. She appeared to be deeply immersed in her thoughts. Seeing her impassive, Ira came near, "It is a beautiful station, isn't it, Madam?"

"We heard that an engineer had built it for his beloved, and in the process, he lost his job."

The lady teacher was still absorbed in her thoughts. Her eyes were moist, she seemed to hear what Ira had said and a tear dropped.

❖ ❖ ❖

OTHER RAIL STORIES

The Tiger Hill Files

The evening was slowly casting its shadow on the railway siding of the Tiger Hill Colliery. It was the month of September, and there was a slight nip in the air. On such a balmy evening, with everything business as usual, Jethuram was reported missing from the siding.

Jethuram was the second fireman in the pilot train to Tiger Hill. The first fireman, Abdul Rehman; the driver, Peter Adams and the guard, Ratnakar Nayak together reported Jethuram's disappearance in the nearby junction of Daritolla.

On the control phone, Peter spoke to the Section Controller. "Hello, Control! After attaching the load of forty box wagons in the siding of Tiger Hill, I created the vacuum and increased the steam of the engine. Jethuram went to attend nature's call to the nearby jungle. But he did not return after the load was ready. I told the guard, and we waited for about an hour before deciding to report the matter at the Daritolla Junction."

The Section Controller noted the details of the case and then asked, "Where do you think Jethuram could have gone?

"Perhaps a tiger caught him."

"What? A tiger?"

Rattled by this possibility, the Section Controller left his cabin in a hurry to inform the Dy CHC, CHC and Loco Controller. The control office suddenly burst into a flurry of noises—anxious murmurs, hushed chatter. The CHC then passed on the preliminary information to the Divisional Operating Superintendent (DOS),

Divisional Mechanical Engineer (DME), RPF Commandant, and Divisional Superintendent (DS).

The news spread like wildfire from station to station, division office to head office in Garden Reach, Kolkata. "*Jethuram has fallen prey to a tiger in the Tiger Hill!*" Fear gripped the locals around Tiger Hill and Doman Hill. The railway staff was reluctant to take the pilot train to the area. The Division Office found itself in a predicament.

The year was 1981, when steam engines were the mainstay, and diesel and electric engines were a rarity. At the time, I was the Assistant Operating Superintendent (AOS) of the division. I had been posted to the Division after completing my training a year ago. I was still new to the railways. The idealism of youth burnt within me, combined with a strong motivation to impress the bosses with good work. Already, I had written the DS's speech for Independence Day celebrations, which he had appreciated. After that, he had assigned me the enquiry of a goods train derailment. He was impressed with my enquiry report and praised it in front of other officers. Naturally, then, I became the first choice for conducting the preliminary enquiry of Jethuram's missing incident. The DS asked me to first file the FIR in the nearby Bijuri Police station and then submit the report.

***

In the first phase of the enquiry, I visited Jethuram's residence. Paying condolences to the bereaved family, on behalf of the railways, was also one of my duties. Jethuram's house was located in the driver's colony in Bilaspur. It was a Type-I staff quarter, with an asbestos roof. The quarter had a veranda in the front, a bedroom in the middle, and a veranda at the back, with the kitchen occupying one end and the bathroom the other.

Jethuram's father was sitting on the charpoy, his amputated perched leg on it and the other leg dangling down. From inside the house, I could hear sounds of wailing. Jethuram's young wife was lying on the floor, her unkempt hair circling her dishevelled tear-stricken face. One woman was sitting beside her and consoling. Jethuram's mother carried her crying infant granddaughter in her arms, patting her gently.

"This is AOS Sahib," the Inspector accompanying me declared by way of introducing me to Jethuram's father, who nodded silently at me.

"Did your son have any enmity with anyone?" I asked.

"No, Sahib. Not at all."

"Was there any quarrel between your son and his wife?"

"None, Sahib."

"Did your son have a drinking problem?"

"No, Sahib. My son was a gem of a person."

A dark shadow of grief clouded the father's face and I did not have the heart to probe any further. Meanwhile, a crowd from the residents of the colony had gathered around us.

Jethuram's old mother came and pleaded with us to trace him out. "How will the family survive?"

"We're doing our best to find him out." Having uttered these words of platitude, I left.

***

Later, I called the driver, the guard, and the first fireman of the pilot train to the Division meeting room for enquiry. Stenographer Durga Rao typed out their statements.

"Peter, that day after reaching Tiger Hill, what did you do?"

"We placed the empty rake on Line 1. The loaded rake was on Line 2. After the load was attached, I created the vacuum and increased the steam of the engine."

"How was the weather that day?"

"It was drizzling."

"Was Jethuram present during the rake placement?"

"Yes, Sahib."

"And after that, where did he go?"

"He told me 'nature calls' and then went into the bushes. But he did not return."

"Tell me … where do you think he might have gone?"

"Sahib, I suspect a tiger has him."

"Why do say that?"

"I heard the roar of a tiger, Sahib."

"Why didn't you go looking for him?"

"It was pitch dark and raining. We were afraid we would get attacked as well, so we all stayed put."

"Have you ever seen a tiger in this area?"

"No, Sahib."

"Who else was there in the siding, besides you, that evening?'

"Nobody. The labourers and colliery supervisors had left the place after loading the rakes."

After the drivers' statements were recorded, the first fireman was asked the same questions. Rehman was a young man in his thirties. His replies matched with that of the driver. He, too, said that he had heard the roar of a tiger. Next up was Ratnakar Nayak, the guard. He, too, was in his thirties. Nayak was a native of Odisha.

I asked Nayak, "What did you do after reaching the Tiger Hill siding?"

He referred to his journal and gave me the timing of the train's arrival, its placement, and the timing of the drawing out.

"How was the weather that day?"

"Cloudy. And it was drizzling a little."

"Did you see Jethuram in the siding?"

"Yes, Sahib! He was there till the load was attached."

"Do you know where he went after that?"

"No Sahib. Peter told us that he went to attend nature's call. I went to check the load by walking from engine to brake van. Abdul and Peter both say that they heard a tiger roar.'

"Did you?"

"No, Sahib. The clouds were rumbling. They must have mistaken that for a tiger's roar."

"Does the rumbling of a cloud sound like the roar of a tiger?"

He smiled a little. "A poet once said so, Sahib."

"Which poet?"

"Kabi Samrat Upendra Bhanja. He said,

> *'Yellow and black striped clouds*
> *Bump into the mountains,*
> *Their lightning-like flashing teeth*
> *Sound like the roar of a tiger.'"*

The lines were in Odia, but I could not fully understand the words despite knowing the language. Nayak explained them as a metaphor between the rumbling of a cloud and the growl of a tiger.

I smiled to myself and asked, "Do you believe that a tiger has taken away Jethuram?"

"Sahib, I am not sure. But since the name of the place is Tiger Hill, people out here must have spotted tigers."

"Have you ever seen a tiger?'

"No, Sahib."

"When did you realize that Jethuram had not returned?"

"Peter stopped the train at Daritolla and broke the news."

"What did you find when you went to check the train?"

"I checked the hot axle, hanging rod, uneven loading, and the vacuum. After the whistle blew, I showed the green light to start the train."

***

After all the statements had been recorded, I took the passport size photo of Jethuram from the Division Office, made copies, and instructed the office to paste it on major railway platforms. A notice was sent to the local newspapers at Bilaspur with photos of the missing person.

Jethuram's father was a gangman of railways. While in service, he had met with an accident and lost a leg. After he was declared unfit for a railway job, his son had got the job as a second fireman on compassionate grounds. At the time of joining, Jethuram was twenty years old, in good health. He was a good football player too. The main job of the second fireman was to feed the engine with coal from the coal tender. One year into the job of pushing coal into the engine had made Jethuram even more sinewy than he was before.

To inspect the site, I took a saloon and camped at Bijuri. Accompanying me was Traffic Inspector Adishesaya. First, I went to Tiger Hill. During British rule, the distance between Rewa and Bilaspur was covered with a dense forest. In those days, tigers roamed freely in the jungles. However, thanks to the shikar expeditions of the British officials and the countryside kings of Ambikapur and Raigarh, those tigers, as well as other wild animals, had been wiped off the face of this part of the country. After coal mines were discovered in the first half of the twentieth century, the lush and dense jungles were also cleared. Only bushes, shrubs and a few sal and kendu trees remained standing, like sentinels. The name "Tiger Hill" became a misnomer, as there was no trace of tigers or hills or even a jungle.

Before this, I had visited the wildlife sanctuaries of Kanha-Kisli, Bandhavgarh, and Panna. Those have thick forests surrounding acres and acres of grassland. Such landscape helped the herbivorous animals to multiply their brood, which also served the tiger population. Tiger Hill did not have such an ecosystem. That is why I found it unlikely that Jethuram had fallen prey to a tiger. While the adjoining Rewa jungle was known to be home to some tigers, it was situated more than a hundred kilometres away, with towns and cities spread in between. That a tiger would travel such a distance, crossing human habitats along the way, sounded a bit farfetched.

The information I gathered from the managers of collieries, mine workers, and some residents was that nobody had sighted a tiger in the recent past, nor had anyone been injured by any tiger attack. A few workers did, however, suggest that some people practised human sacrifices in a temple in Doman Hill. They suspected that Jethuram might have been abducted for a sacrifice.

Doman Hill was situated close to Tiger Hill. During the British era, it was called Demon Hill, because the prehistoric tribal inhabitants practised human sacrifice. A Britisher called John Honda once went missing and was later found to have fallen prey to human sacrifice. Over time, the name Demon Hill was distorted to Doman hill. Education permeated the tribal communities, with many people being deployed as workers in the mines of Korea-Rewa. It seemed fair to assume that the primitive practice of human sacrifice must have become a thing of the past.

Another rumour I heard among the railway employees of Bijuri was that Jethuram might have fallen victim to the charms of some "banjaran" temptress. There were many stories that told of nomadic tribes, who were experts in burglary. Their women supposedly had the power to lure young men. I had seen these banjaras pitching their tents near the stations of Bilaspur, Anuppur, and Sahdol. They would display their wares for sale—bear nails, beaks of some exotic birds, reptile skin, dead chameleon—along with rare herbs, roots, and barks of medicinal plants, which they claimed had curative properties. The banjara's claim to have found a panacea for impotency, sterility, and snake bites had found acceptance among villagers who used to buy such magic potions as a remedy for their illnesses. To me, they appeared simple folks, so Jethuram's elopement with any one of the banjarans, leaving behind his young wife and family and a stable railway job, did not sound convincing to me.

***

I submitted my preliminary enquiry report to the DS. I mentioned that Jethuram's vanishing act was indeed mysterious. The

DS then instructed me to follow up with the police investigation. The fact that Jethuram was a Class-IV employee of the railways was probably the reason why his disappearance did not invoke much interest with the police authorities. They had not even initiated the process of enquiry.

The DS took up the matter with the SP and prodded him to start the investigation soon, for the simple reason that any delay may have a negative impact on the morale of the railway employees. Consequently, one inspector and two constables were assigned to the case, who camped in the Tiger Hill Colliery Guest House. Accompanying them were two dogs. The two dogs were adorned in winter clothing and generated considerable intrigue. A crowd assembled in Tiger Hill to see the dogs. Leaving behind their job of loading coal, the workers became curious onlookers. Joining them were the stray dogs of the area, who found their richer brethren strange and quirky. Wherever the police dogs moved in around the bushes and alleys, sniffing things around, the stray dogs and the workers followed. The constables soon tired of managing the locals and opened blank fire to disperse the gathering.

Three more days passed. The police camp made some feeble attempts, but no leads were found in the case. The disappearance of Jethuram became one more cold case in the police file.

***

A few months after this incident, one ghastly carnage happened in the mine area. In the areas of Tiger Hill, Doman Hill, Bijuri, Kotma, thirty people succumbed after consuming spurious country liquor. Some forty people were admitted to the hospitals at Bishrampur, Manendragarh, and Chirimiri in very serious conditions.

Panic spread in the mining area of Korea-Rewa. The excise and police department of the government swung into action and cracked down on the liquor barons of the area. The affected people gave the names of two or three businessmen related to the trade. Raghab Sharma was the liquor trader of the Tiger Hill area, while Rebati Verma operated from Doman Hill. When their houses were raided, it was found that they, too, had succumbed to the poison. Their houses echoed with pitiable cries.

Chandrabhanu Shah was a big trader in Kotma mining area. When the police went to look for him, they found him absconding. After some days, his dead body washed up on the banks of the Hasdeo river. The investigation team could not book anyone for the hooch tragedy, so to make a show of their capability, the police constables caught hold of a vagabond who used to roam near the Bijuri bus stand, singing in praise of drinking. Many kicks and butts later, it transpired that he was a madcap.

For a few days, the government's inability to find the miscreants made headlines in the local newspapers and became the subject of heated discussions in the state assembly. In response, a few excise department officers were suspended, and the story was given a quiet burial.

***

A strange incident took place in the Khongsara-Bhanwartonk section some months after the liquor incident. A horde of elephants occupied the rail tracks between the stations of Khongsara and Bhanwartonk. The horde consisted of twenty elephants, including the baby ones. The elephants were playfully prancing around the railway tracks, as if under the spell of mahuli, the country liquor. The two sides of the railway tracks were thicketed with mahul trees. It was later discovered that the breweries were closeted inside those thick forests into which the excise department had never made any inroads. The elephant horde was attracted to the smell emanating from the mahuli breweries and had invaded the railway tracks for their merrymaking. Passenger trains and goods train had to be stopped for six hours for such a rail *roko* move by the wild animals.

After the incident, about ten Bhil tribal people were caught and interrogated by the police.

"Since when have you been making country liquor?"

"Since many years, Sahib. This is our livelihood."

"Do you supply the liquor outside?"

"Yes, Huzoor."

"How?"

"By train."

"Passenger train or goods train?"

"Goods train, Sahib."

"Do you travel with it yourselves?"

"No, Sahib. We send it with the railway people."

"Which railway people?"

"One gora sahib takes it. He has two assistants with him."

"They freight it every day?"

"No, Sahib. Once a week, two or three times they work on the goods train. The day the Sahib is on duty on the goods train, he signals us. We bring the barrels near the rail line."

"How does he send signals?"

"From a distance away, he whistles. First four short whistles. Then one long whistle. Like this, if we hear three continuous three whistles, we carry the barrels to the train line. He stops the train and loads the barrels to the rail wagons. The driver then offloads some coal for us and settles our money."

"Do you know the name of this, Sahib?"

"No, Sahib. His subordinates call him 'master'."

"How does he look?"

"White, like chalk, with a moustache and a beard."

"How old?"

"Over forty, Sahib."

"And the others accompanying him?"

"Two natives. Youngish."

The Police SP sought the assistance of the DS as the hooch business had links with railway staff. The DS then delegated the task to me.

***

To know how many staff members were on duty in this section in the past six months, I called for the roster of the guards and drivers from the office of the Foreman and the Yard Master. I did a study of the T-34 HF journals prepared by the guards and the control charts. A thorough examination of these records revealed a pattern. As per the working timetable, the goods train ought to take twenty minutes between Khongsara and Bhanwartonk. But some trains were taking an additional eight to ten minutes. The guards were reporting "loco loss: driver to explain" in the T34-HF journal.

Though different guards were posted in these trains, the driver remained the same. It was Peter Adams, the Anglo-Indian driver from Bilaspur, whom I had interviewed after Jethuram's disappearance. I called for his logbook. He had justified the extra time taken thus: "Train stalling due to heavy up gradient, engine not able to haul."

From the booking register, the details of firemen assisting him were found. In most of the trips, the first fireman was Rehman, and the second fireman was Jethuram. Further investigation revealed that during Peter's duty, the consumption of coal was one tonne extra on each trip. My suspicion grew. *He must be the one supplying coal to the tribals.* Peter Adam's involvement in the hooch trading became evident like daylight.

By the time the police went to nab Peter and his assistant, Tukaram, they had all disappeared. They had got wind of the investigation after the control records and loco booking office were seized. Tukaram was caught from his relatives from Sahdol. He confessed to having collaborated with Peter in the liquor trading. He revealed that he was getting fifty rupees per trip from Peter.

After some days, the police nabbed Rehman from Bareilly in UP. He had taken refuge at his in-laws' place. During the interrogation, he confessed about his involvement in the liquor trading. He admitted his crime and agreed to become the main approver in the case.

Before Jethuram's disappearance, Rehman and Peter were fully involved in the liquor trading. I had a suspicion that Rehman and Peter were behind the disappearance of Jethuram. So I requested the SP to re-open the file of Jethuram.

The investigation took a different turn now. As per CrPC164,

Rehman's confessions were recorded.

"You were supplying liquor from Bhanwartonk to Korea-Rewa?"

"Yes, Sahib."

"Was it part of your railway duty?"

"No, Sahib. It was a grave mistake."

"Then why were you doing this?"

"Peter had tempted us."

"Were the guards involved in this business?"

"No, Sahib. The guards are in the brake van after forty wagons. They have no idea about anything."

"You stopped the train between Bhanwartonk and Khongsara and supplied coal to the tribal people?"

"Yes, Sahib."

"Your department did not know about this?"

"Master was reporting that more coal is being used due to the steep incline in the section."

"Was Jethuram involved in this?"

"Yes, Sahib."

"So where did Jethuram go?"

"I can't say, Sahib."

"Was there any quarrel between you three about this liquor trade?"

Suddenly, Rehman jumped up, looking around in concern.

The investigating Police Inspector stopped the enquiry and took him to the nearby room. After some time, he was brought back to the main room with his dress and hair in a dishevelled state.

"Now, will you tell us the truth? If you do, we will reduce your punishment."

Hesitantly, Rehman began:

"That day, we had taken six barrels of liquor to Tiger Hill. All along the way, Jethuram was yapping. 'Master don't do this work anymore. One day we will get caught. We are getting our daily bread from the railways. Let us not betray the railways. We are stealing coal. That is not right ...' Master got annoyed and yelled, 'Shut up you Jethuram! You are getting your share, na?' But Jethuram kept pleading, saying if he lost his job, his family will not survive. Master assured Jethuram that if he kept quiet, he would make him rich. But Jethuram was not to be silenced. As the traders unloaded the barrels at Tiger Hill, he kept saying, 'Master, promise me this is the last time you will do this. If you don't, I will report to Loco Foreman.' Master lost his temper at this threat. He shouted, 'Such audacity! You scoundrel, son of a pig!' Then, in a rage, Master hit his head with a shovel. Jethuram collapsed. Seeing this, my blood clammed up. I said, 'Master what did you do? He is not breathing.' Master threatened me too. 'You keep quiet,' he said. 'Do what I tell you to do. Hold his legs.' I did as I was told. 'Where will we take him?' I asked. Master smiled and said, 'No need to take him anywhere.' Then he inserted Jethuram's head in the mouth of the engine, pushed the body, and closed the shutter. Master said, 'The fire will destroy all evidence. Nobody can catch us now. If anyone asks, you tell them that Jethuram has been taken away by a tiger.'"

Rehman paused, drank some water, then continued. "The earth under my feet was sinking, Sahib. I simply sat down holding my throbbing head. From that side of the engine, a putrid smell was coming. Master opened the shutter and shoved some more coal into the burning fire." Suddenly, Rehman burst out sobbing.

I was stupefied. Can greed make a human stoop to such levels?

Composing myself, I asked, "Did the guard come to know about it?"

"No, Sahib. He was checking the train."

Now that we knew that Peter was the main culprit behind

Jethuram's disappearance and the hooch tragedy, a high alert was issued to nab him.

As per Railway Pass declaration, Peter's family consisted of his wife and a son. However, they had emigrated to Australia a while back. In the Anglo-Indian colony in Bilaspur, only a handful of Anglo-Indian railway employees resided. Most of them had migrated to Australia. Peter had a Chhattisgarhi lady as the caretaker of his living quarters. She was not able to give us any information regarding Peter.

A red alert was issued to all the international airports in the country. On gathering from intelligence sources that Peter had collected his Visa and booked a ticket with Air India, Bilaspur police sent its forces to the Delhi Airport. After the third and final call of the Air India flight was announced, a suited–booted, clean-shaven person emerged from the bathroom and took hurried strides towards the immigration gate. The person resembled a corporate executive. His bearing was sophisticated. He was just one step away from the immigration entry when a few policemen in plain clothes blocked his path and flashed their cards. "Mr Peter Adams, you are under arrest."

Draupadi

The Ahmedabad-Howrah Express halted at Surat station. It was a two-minute stoppage. A couple with dented trunks on their heads and cloth bags in the crooks of their arm, running breathless, just about managed to enter a compartment. From their attire, they appeared to be manual workers. Seeing them, a passenger at the door scoffed, "Hey you! Don't get in here. This is reserved."

The couple ignored the scorn, wriggled in, and found a place near the bathroom. They placed their tin trunks on the floor and sat down on them. They did not go inside to check for seats—as if the place near the bathroom was allotted to them. With great trepidation, the man—Hazari—asked the passenger on the aisle seat, "Will this train go via Odisha?" The passenger uttered a perfunctory "yes" and turned his face, as if the couple's presence was an irritant. A glimmer of relief crossed Hazari's wrinkled face. His wife, Kajali, stayed silent.

The train chugged along from Surat, and soon, as is the norm, the Travelling Ticket Examiner (TTE) started his round of mandatory ticket-checking. Seeing Hazari and Kajali nicely ensconced on the trunk, the TTE got irked—like an Alsatian when a cow enters the sahib's premises. He scowled, "Hey! This is the sleeper class. Get out of here."

"Babu I have the tickets," Hazari entreated.

"Arre … these are general tickets. You cannot get a berth in this compartment with these."

"Babu, we don't want seats. We are sitting on our trunks."

"So what? You are in the compartment." The TTE sounded angry.

Hazari started pleading in his broken Hindi. "Riots broken out in Surat, Sir. All workers fleeing the place … trains all packed … not an inch to get a foothold. Myself going home with my woman. Pardon my mistake, Babu."

The TTE took out a receipt book from his black coat. "Okay, if you want to go on this train you have to pay a fine of rupees one hundred and six, each."

"Where will I get so much money, Babu? My shack was burnt in the riots; whatever little was there has turned into ash. With great difficulty, we sold our utensils and got this ticket."

"Ok, if not one hundred and six, then at least give fifty-eight each."

"Babu … not even a rupee I have on me."

"Such a bunch of liars!" exclaimed the TTE. "The same story every time. No money. Then why do you get out of your place in the first place? Are the Railways your in-laws?" Hazari was going on making pitiable sounds when the TTE clinched the matter with an air of finality. "This won't do! I'm getting the TTE squad." With that, the man exited the compartment through the vestibule connector.

After a while, he came back with other TTEs from the TTE squad, along with hammals. From the stout bodies and thick moustache of the hammals, they looked like the thugs from old grandma stories. They were carrying sticks and brandished them in front of Hazari for good measure. Yet, the fine could not be extracted out of him.

The squad-in-charge ordered one hammal, "Take him to the bathroom and search him." Promptly, Hazari was taken to the bathroom. His dhotis, his underwear, the lining with hidden pockets—everything was thoroughly searched. But it was all in vain.

After a while, Hazari came out of the bathroom, sobbing silently. He was shaken. Such insult—and in front of his wife!

Sitting on the trunk, awestruck Kajali was watching the drama from inside her ghunghat. When she saw Hazari, she gasped. As she moved her hands to cover her mouth, her bangles tinkled audibly.

The TTE turned around. "Arre! Your woman has all the money. Better take it out from her, huh!"

Hazari was now desperate. His sobs grew louder. "Babu! Kick me, slap me, beat me. Do whatever you want with me. But do not touch my woman. I swear, Babu, we have no money to go up to the village or eat."

One hammal said, "Sir, it is all dramabazi. Shall we search the woman?"

The TTE pondered before replying, "No, no ... the situation will get out of hand. Do not touch the woman. Give a message to the next station. Let a lady TTE come and search her. Surely, she has the money. See the heavy silver ornaments she is wearing on her nose and hands."

"Okay, Sir!" the hammals responded in unison.

All this while, the other passengers in the compartment remained unmoved and indifferent. A game of cards was going on in the adjacent seat.

It was soon time for the next stop, Bhusaval, the city of bananas and oranges. It was a good fifteen minutes halt.

Hazari's heart was pounding. *What will happen now? Will they come and harass us again? When will my trials end? What will I do? What will happen to Kajali?* A loudspeaker nearby was belching out a Hindi film tune, "*Choli ke pichhe kya hai! Choli ke pichhe ...*"

At Bhusaval, the squad members returned with a lady TTE. The team was clearly recharged and knew their mission well. From Kajali's silver ornaments, their attention now shifted to her red blouse—an old-moth-smelly piece that clung to her slender body. Huddled on the trunk, Kajali sensed the collective gaze. Her hands instinctively moved to her chest, in a bid to cover the treasure trove.

The crowd in the compartment became vicariously expectant.

The male TTE apprised the lady TTE of the situation and what was expected from her. She took one look at Kajali. *Such a poor woman, with a mere few silver ornaments, conspicuous on her slender arms*, the lady TTE thought. A storm was brewing in her head. She knew how it was to come from a poor background; she had come from one herself. *No*, she thought. She could not search Kajali in front of such a rapacious crowd. So she walked up to Kajali, hoping to cajole her. As she inched closer, Kajali thought the woman with the black coat was another "Dushasan" out to disrobe her.

Hazari stood stupefied. The members of the squad and other hammals were in a charged mood. The passengers in the compartment got out of their cocoons and became quiet spectators. Even the passing chaiwallahs and kelawallahs on the platform stopped in their tracks and started peeping inside. The loudspeaker was mercilessly belching out: "*Choli ke pichhe kya hai. Choli ke pichhe.*"

Then all of a sudden, Kajali jumped into the ring of hammals with a jig and a war cry. In her half-Hindi, half-Odia she screamed, "All you Yamadutas! Don't you have mothers or sisters? You have no one but these poor people to harass? Are all the travellers going with tickets? Why don't you check the rich? Why do you let them go? Why do you treat us like dogs and monkeys?" Like a demoness, she lashed out, "Which Father's son will disrobe me? Who wants to see what is inside my choli? Take this!" Enraged, Kajali tore open the red blouse and threw it at the Lady TTE.

The curious onlookers, with gaping expectant eyes, would have noticed a desert land—only a plateau, with no mountains. It was a place that had seen neither spring nor autumn, nor even rains. Neither flowers nor fruits had ever blossomed in that desert land. Her bony arms outstretched, Kajali shook her arms, jingling her bangles in the process. "This is all that I have, you swines! These bangles are all my wealth, my shield—and they protect me from all evils you monsters!"

The squad was turning their face to shoo away the crowd.

The Lady TTE threw back the choli to her in a bid to cover her. Then she made a receipt and handed it over to Kajali. "Go, no one can fine you now." The loudspeaker was still blaring "*Choli ke pichhe kya he … Choli ke pichhe …*"

A quietened Kajali was still dangling her bangles when the whistle of the train blew.

Big Boss Comes to Town

The wire from the Kolkata HQ sounded ominous. The head of our department (HOD) would be visiting our division. The stated reason: "Loading in the mining area has considerably reduced." The steel factories had been raising a huge hue and cry regarding the disruption in the supply of raw materials. So, the HOD was to investigate the matter on the spot, and he was meeting the mining barons of the area.

Like all bosses, the HOD too had a hidden agenda. It was common knowledge that the jungles of western Odisha fascinated the HOD, which explained his periodic visits to this area. And this time too, he was being accompanied by his family—his wife and only daughter. Two days were earmarked for his visit to our division.

My immediate superior got started on the arrangements required for the visit: how the saloon will come from Kolkata, where it will be parked, what guesthouse the HOD will stay in, how many cars and jeeps will be engaged in his service. No wonder he had acquired a reputation for being adept at such official *bandobast*. It was decided that the saloon would be parked at Nuamundi station. From there, the VIP would go and stay in the guesthouse of the steel plant. The nearby places were full of tourist spots, like the *Murga Mahadev Mandir*, the Handidhua falls, and the tribal *bastis*—good entertainment for the HOD's wife. The assigned vehicles would be parked there for the entire duration of their visit.

After all the arrangements were made, my superior called me. "Listen, I have not been keeping well. You may have to accompany the HOD in my place." Then, my superior launched into a tirade about the HOD. "You know, Mr Verma is a living legend in the Operating Department and enjoys a formidable reputation for being a taskmaster. His reputation precedes him, and his mere presence is enough to create a stir among the hawkers, porters, and other staff."

I sensed danger. I had joined the railways only a year ago. To handle the tour programme for such a high-ranking official seemed daunting. I felt very distressed.

***

One day before the arrival of the HOD, I camped in Nuamundi with my team. The HOD was supposed to leave Kolkata in the night and reach Nuamundi by early morning. The HOD's itinerary spread like bushfire among the constituents; every staff member knew it. The yard, cabins, and platforms were suddenly full of life. Month-old cobwebs were removed from the station rooms, grass and weeds were uprooted from the platforms, all pending records were set right, and all staff members—even those that never wore their uniforms—somehow managed to fit themselves into their discarded ones. On the day of the HOD's arrival, Nuamundi station was decked up like a bride. With expectation and apprehension, we all waited for him to come.

Mr Verma was the first one to step out of the train. I had had no opportunity to meet him before. A North Indian, tall and stout, he sported a long handlebar moustache. The white strands of hair on his head declared the onset of old age—perhaps his late fifties. Mrs Verma was much younger. Added to that, the *salwar-kameez* attire successfully hid her real age, so much so that I did not hazard a guess. The cynosure of all eyes, however, was the daughter. Slim, fair, and pretty, she too was attired in fashionable ethnic wear. In between the two beauties, the HOD looked like a beast.

Once Mr Verma set his foot on the platform, we all rushed to greet him with the customary flower bouquets. Without giving us so much as a second glance, his eyes started scanning the entire spectrum of the platform to assess the reason for such a crowd. He called me aside and, in a rather harsh but low voice, enquired, "Who are these jokers?" Before I could clear my throat to give a fitting explanation, some gentlemen from the crowd thrust their bouquets towards him. I had no option but to go through the routine of introductions.

"This is Mr Sharma, Director of Mining Corporation."

"This here is Mr Raja Reddy, General Manager of the nearby cement factory."

"And this, Mr Raghabendra Mahapatra, mining baron."

Those that I did not know personally introduced themselves. In the meantime, the HOD's luggage had been carted to the car. The people who had come to pay their obeisance also returned to their vehicles.

Once we were settled in the car and on our way, Mr Verma turned to me and said, "What was this, Mister? Did you call the meeting on the platform itself?"

"No, Sir. The meeting will be at the guesthouse."

"Then why such a big procession of people out here? They could have come to the guesthouse."

"No, Sir! They came on their own … to welcome you. Sir, it is difficult to keep the news from spreading when such a big officer comes to this small place."

Then came a barrage of the choicest invectives: useless, incompetent, waster … anything his fertile mind could think of. On that cold winter morning, I could feel the perspiration under my neck. To add insult to injury, his wife and daughter were suppressing their giggles at my discomfiture.

***

The meeting was fixed for 11 a.m. I was prepared one hour before and waited at the lounge of the guesthouse. At around 12, the HOD climbed down the red-carpeted staircase with a briefcase in his hand. I rushed forward to help him with the case, but he moved away and yelled, 'What is this? Are you a peon that you are scampering to carry the briefcase for me?'

The guesthouse staff, the drivers … everyone was in the lounge. The HOD's daughter was waving at him from the balcony. In front of such a crowd, his harsh words hit me hard. All my upbringing, which taught me to respect elders by carrying their baggage, had been laid to waste in front of a crowd by this belligerent boss.

After the meeting, a customary lunch had been arranged. A motley crowd of participating officers, besides a handful of dignitaries who came with their wives, made up the crowd along with other invitees—making the luncheon quite a formal affair. Mr Verma was accompanied by his wife.

Later, the lunch party turned into a drinks party. At that point of time, I had not yet developed a taste for such indulgences. The whole thing seemed like a waste of time, with people holding their shots and pegs, munching on nuts and savouries, making small talk about Spain to Siberia. I felt like a fish out of water. With a soft drink in hand, I sat in a corner, trying to make myself invisible, when the Boss' Utpal Dutt-like round eyes fell on me.

Walking up to me, he said, "What young man! Sitting with a cold drink?"

"I have never touched hard drinks, Sir."

"Then start today."

"No, Sir. Please excuse me. I can't."

"Why? Have you kept some vow or what? Like the Bhisma Pitamah?" With that, he broke out in a guffaw, the booming laughter reverberating in the dining hall. It infected the entire crowd. Everyone's gaze fell on me. I became red in embarrassment.

"Will you shame the railways? Come, come, hold the glass."

The HOD's action created a chain reaction. Many of the officers rallied with him, surrounding me. One officer cooked up an alcoholic concoction and brought it to me.

Mr Verma spoke again. "See, even ladies are drinking."

Despite all my protest, the drink was poured down my throat. It was nauseating. I felt like I was being ragged.

At the first opportunity, I left the party and returned to my room. My skin crawled and a seething rage formed inside me thinking about how the HOD had treated me.

***

The next day was reserved for the "pleasure trip." The HOD loved hunting. He had already given instructions for arrangements to be made for a *shikar*. A well-known hunter named Bimbadhar was drafted, who had been Mr Verma's shikar companion since the latter's heydays. The programme was chalked out. After an early dinner, he would go out with Bimbadhar to Saranda jungle. The jeep was ready. Mrs Verma accompanied him.

I pretended to be sick to avoid meeting him.

My job in the railways, with endless work and never-satisfied bosses, their shouting and screaming over phones, seemed no better than the lecturer's job I had left behind. What had attracted me to the job was my wanderlust—my desire to travel from Kashmir to Kanyakumari. But it made my mother sad, since I had to leave home. And now, even I was distressed beyond words. A storm was raging inside me.

After much reflection, I sat down to draft my resignation letter.

Thak! Thak! Thak!

The knock at the door interrupted my process. I put the letter inside my shirt pocket and stood up to open the door. At the door stood the HOD's daughter, with a jasmine-like smile on her face. But even such a radiant smile was not enough to wipe out the agony in my heart. *Has she come to add salt to the wounds inflicted by her father?* I wondered.

"Yes, Miss Verma?"

My own voice sounded strange to me.

"My name is Suman."

"Okay, Suman. Please tell me why you are here."

"Please come for dinner. The cook and servants have all retired.

Food has already been served for the two of us in the dining hall."

"Thank you, but I am not hungry."

"How come? At lunchtime, too, you did not eat properly."

"Why does that bother you?"

"I feel that you are annoyed … perhaps."

Then, much to my shock, she grabbed my hand and pulled me towards the dining hall. An unknown girl holding my hand … it was such a novel experience for me, I was rendered speechless.

At the dining table, she served me one dish after another. I ate, slowly and reluctantly, with the anguish still brewing inside me.

"Daddy misbehaved with you today. I feel very sorry. But please don't misunderstand him. He's not a bad man. That is just his style."

This set me off. "Whatever I had heard about your father before, he is many times worse than that."

"What do you mean?"

"When he arrived, some people went to the station to greet him. He should have been happy. Instead, he was angry. Then, when he was going for the meeting, out of respect, I wanted to hold the briefcase for him. He berated me. And finally, despite me telling him that I do not drink, he forced it on me in front of so many people!"

Suman giggled and her sparkling laughter surprised me. "Please try to understand from my father's perspective," she said. "You should have realized that, since he has come with family, you need not have made the introductory session at the platform so long. Secondly, you are a class one officer of the central government. To run to pick up someone's briefcase does not behove of your status. Your subordinates would not have found it dignified. And finally, it's okay if you don't drink, but you could at least hold a glass in such a social setting. Even if you don't like alcohol, drinking once in a blue moon will not bring the sky down."

A girl of no more than twenty, at least five years younger to me, giving me such sermons … it was beyond my imagination. I kept my gaze fixed on the food plate. After I had finished my meal, I managed to utter a gentle thank you and returned to my room.

****

The moonlit night was still young. The light trickled in as if someone was sprinkling moondust from the window. I was trying to catch some sleep. The boss and his daughter were alternately invading my thoughts. One was like burning sunrays and the other like the cool rays of the moon.

In that half-dreamy and half-asleep state, Suman appeared every inch a pious Vedic lady—the likes of Gargi, Maitreyee. I was sitting with her disciples at the graduation ceremony of the hermitage and listening to her sermons about facing the big bad world. The resignation letter lying in my pocket was interrupting my dream-like visions. I woke up as if in a trance, tore the letter into shreds, and threw it out of the window. The pieces flew away, flapping their wings like birds. The sound of their wings cleared the cobwebs of my mind.

It must have been the wee hours of the morning when I heard the horn of a car outside. The sound of footsteps followed. They were getting closer, and then … *knock, knock*!

I opened the door. It was the office driver.

"Sir! Bada Sahib is calling. He has returned with a catch of a rooster. Nobody is there in the guesthouse to serve him. He has ordered to call the cooks. The rooster has to be roasted, Sir!"

"Go and tell him that I am not his peon. This is my sleeping time. Tell him not to disturb me."

The dawn was slowly breaking on the eastern sky.

Casabianca

The Palasa–Gunupur passenger train's empty rake logged on to the platform of Palasa. Soon, a scramble for the empty seats ensued among the waiting passengers. Biju and I threw our bags from outside on to the window seats. That was the usual practice to get them "reserved," so to say. A seat in the passenger train was preferable to a bus seat, which was not only costlier but also painfully bumpy on the dilapidated and potholed roads of this border town, Palasa, lying between Odisha and Andhra Pradesh. According to Biju, the passenger train always ran packed house, but at the originating station and early in the morning, we could get those two coveted seats without much ado.

In those wee hours of 3 in the morning, the light bulbs on the platform, placed in most obscure corners, were trying unsuccessfully to mitigate the thick darkness around. Inside the compartment, the lights were so dim that we could hardly see anything except a vague apparition of our seats. We placed our bags on the upper seat and spread ourselves on the two window seats facing each other. Life was comfortable. The hustle bustle of the platform had started to fade away. As the train chugged along, sleep overcame us.

***

When we opened our eyes, dawn had already broken. The skies were bright. I got up and stretched myself fully when something soft hit my legs under the seat. *Somebody must have kept his luggage underneath*, I thought.

I called out to Biju. "Oy, has someone kept a sack or something under my seat?"

Biju knelt down and immediately screamed, "A dog! A dog!"

"*Arre sala* …!" I got up with a jerk and looked under the seat. A dog it was! Black, shoe-faced, with two long ears falling on both sides of the face, like two crestfallen snake hoods. The whole body was covered in fur, like a bear. The face was perched on the front legs and the brown eyes were shining like light bulbs.

A dog under the seat can create quite a flutter among bored fellow passengers. Some passengers got up from their seats and came to watch the creature. Comments flew thick and fast.

"This is not a native dog."

"No, looks like some foreign breed."

"But why is it lying quietly under the seat?"

"No movement either. Is he injured?"

I lifted up my legs onto the seat under which the object of curiosity was squatting. It looked like the questions were being directed towards me, as if I was the owner.

"Shh, get up, come on!" I urged the dog.

He did not react and continued to look at me with innocent eyes.

"This is not a street dog. Looks like somebody's pet," Biju said.

"But how did he get here?"

Biju worked in the parcel office of the railways. He said, "Many a time people send parcels without paying the freight. Maybe the owner has not booked the dog and is transporting him free of cost. Whether it is in the guard van or with oneself, the minimum freight is fifty rupees. Maybe the owner wants to cheat the railways of this princely sum."

"The owner must have surely come before the empty rake came. Must be somewhere around. Let us see!"

"Whose dog is this? Whose dog is this?" Biju went up and down the compartment shouting.

There was no response. The dog sat unperturbed and unruffled. As for me, there seemed to be no threat from him, so I relaxed.

***

After a while, the train stopped at one of the bigger stations. A chaiwallah went past, calling, '*Chai garam ... chai garam.*'

I got down from the compartment. When I returned with two plastic cups of tea, I found a vendor selling peanuts, his basket placed on my seat. On seeing me, he politely picked up his basket.

I asked him, 'Listen, one dog is sleeping here. Do you know whose it is?'

"Ah, Sahib, this doggy has been here for a while."

"What? Since when?"

"He is waiting for his master, Sahib. To come and take him."

The peanutwallah moved away as other passengers signalled to him. After I had finished my tea, he returned. "Sahib! Shall I give you some nuts?"

"No! No! Thank you."

The train was starting to move. The hawker calls faded. Biju was back from the platform, making his way to the seat.

I said, "Biju, do you think the owner has deliberately left him?"

"Who knows. Maybe he is sick. See, he is not moving at all."

"Maybe he is old. I once read in a column by Maneka Gandhi that when pet dogs become old and sick, their owners often leave them in deserted places. Those pets miss their owners and without food and water, either die or get mad."

"In foreign countries, when such a thing happens, the owners shoot their pets and relieve them of their pain and suffering ... that is what I have heard," Biju replied grimly.

"But in our country, the owners cleverly absolve themselves from the responsibility. If some NGO adopts them, well and good. Otherwise, their premature death is guaranteed."

A sense of pity surged inside me, not only for this dog but the entire canine fraternity. This canine tribe is such a faithful one. To save their masters, dogs will even sacrifice their lives. In case the master dies before them, some dogs follow them up to their burial ground, sit and mourn their death, or wait for their masters to wake up from the grave.

I felt sad for this dog. I had some biscuits in my bag. I took them out and put a few before him, coaxing him to eat. "Ae Tommy, Ae Rocky…" I called out whatever dog name came to my mind. But the dog did not so much as glance at the offering.

Before long, we reached Parlakhemundi station—our destination.

***

Arrangements had been made for me and Biju to stay in the dak bungalow. I was to attend a literature society meeting as the chief guest. Many known and unknown faces, writers and poets, had gathered there. The soiree went on till late evening. In the end, I went to sleep tired and exhausted.

Next morning, we returned to the Parlakhemundi station to catch the train back home. As usual, the train was packed to capacity. The moment I entered the platform, I remembered the under-the-seat dog.

I reminded Biju, "Let us go and see whether the dog is still in that compartment. That was the last bogie. We may also get a place to sit.'

"Okay, then let us walk ahead. In the return train, the marshalling will be on the opposite end. In case we don't get a seat, I will take you to the guard's brake van."

We walked briskly and entered the first compartment. Lo and

behold! The dog was still there—in the same place, under the same seat. We were amazed. No one was occupying that seat, possibly because of the dog situation.

Biju and I quickly grabbed the same seats. The train whistled and started with a jerk. Biju said, "This dog is of a good breed. Why don't you take him home? You have made a new house. He could be a nice new addition."

"You think he will come? What if he is like Casabianca?"

"What do you mean?"

"Haven't you read the story of Casabianca?"

"No."

"A boy named Casabianca was travelling with his father on a ship. His father had told him to sit on a particular place on the deck. The ship caught fire. But his father hadn't returned, so the boy kept waiting. He didn't leave the burning deck because he did not want to disobey his father's orders. Eventually, he was burnt to death. This dog is also like that. He will not get up from where he has been asked to stay."

Biju didn't say a word, but he looked sad.

To satisfy Biju, I bent down and said, "Doggy, will you come with us?"

The dog closed his eyes upon hearing my words and lay still.

Our old friend, the peanutwallah, surfaced again in our compartment. He was wearing the same loose pants from the day before and a new yellow-striped shirt. He recognized us and smiled. "Namaskar, Sahib."

"Today we will take nuts from you," I said. "Give us in two paper cones."

The peanutwallah made two paper cones and filled them up with nuts.

"Listen," I said, "yesterday you said this dog has been abandoned by his master. What happened to that person?"

"Nothing has happened to him, Sahib. He is hale and hearty. I spotted him in Palasa. He left by Madras Mail."

"How does this man look?"

"Good looking, well-dressed man. The first time he came to the station with the dog, he was wearing a coat. Must be from a rich family."

"Accha, is this dog never hungry or thirsty? I gave him biscuits, but he didn't touch them."

"Sahib, I also offered bread once, but he didn't touch it. Maybe he will eat once his master returns.'

"Then … when you see his master, will you tell him that the dog is waiting for him?"

"No, Sahib. Perhaps this dog has some disease. That is why his master is avoiding him. These days, his master is not seen wearing suits. He is seen in dhoti kurta. Some time back, this dog was following a suited-booted man, but it wasn't his master. Since then, he has been lying here quietly. I think his master is hiding from him. That is why he is changing his clothes. Who knows what the man is up to?"

Having finished his story, the peanutwallah went way. "Peanuts, peanuts … hot … hot … peanuts," he called out in his usual singsong voice.

I looked out of the window. Not very far, a thin strip of a river was visible. From the bosom of the river, rocks jutted out like bones of emaciated, hungry people. Only the water underneath the railway bridge appeared a deep blue. "Biju which river is this?"

"Nagabali," Biju replied from the side seat.

Biju's ancestral place was Parlakhemundi. So he knew the geography of the area intimately.

The river was laced with a paddy field. Storks were flying

across the field, and cranes were lounging by the riverbank. Their white feather could put to shame the attire of any neta. Buffaloes were cooling themselves in the shallow water. The most beautiful were the village belles. Some were soaking in the water; some were carrying pots on their slim waists. The scene could not have been more delightful. I was trying to capture it in my memory, to retrieve and savour later.

The peanutwallah return to our compartment broke my reverie. He bent down to look under my seat. Making a fist and shaking his thumb, he ranted at the dog. "Hey doggy, you think your master will come back? Why are you waiting for his return? He must have already got himself another fancy dog. If you are sane, come out, eat something, and mix with other fellas of your fraternity at the station. Else, go with this Babu who is offering you biscuits. He will keep you in a canine orphanage in Bhubaneswar. Why are you sulking like this?"

Then, with a song on his lips, he moved to the next compartment.

"Devi Ramchandi left the palace to collect water.

Kalapahada kept waiting at the door."

The train started making a clattering sound as it picked up speed on the bridge. Suddenly, the dog emerged from under the seat. He shook his ears and moved towards the door in the direction the peanutwallah had gone. *The peanutwallah's acerbic words must have hurt him*, I thought. *He is out to follow him on a revenge trail.*

But all of a sudden, we heard a loud splash. "What happened? What happened?" Biju yelled. We rushed to the door.

A conundrum had disrupted the peaceful scenery from minutes ago. The birds were flying away from the waterbed. The buffaloes had scattered. A few village belles yelled and dropped their water pots.

Stunned, we kept looking at the whirlpool in the river—at its heart, the shape of a dog.

❖ ❖ ❖

Complaint

Conductor Bholanath Prasad was pacing up and down in front of the Senior Divisional Commercial Manager's room. Ten steps from one side, ten steps from the opposite side—that was the exact space available in front of the room. In full uniform, he presented a neat picture: white trousers and white shirt under the black coat, with matching tie and the identity card proudly hanging on his chest with the inscription "B.N. Prasad, Conductor, South Eastern Railway".

Bholanath had been suspended from his service. This was the day of his enquiry. Hence, his restlessness. He had been rehearsing his oral submission since he received the intimation. Everyone in the division knew that Bholanath was one of the sincere workers. As with all organizations, the Indian Railways also run on the shoulders of a few committed workers—and profitably at that. For such people, work is the first priority and everything else come a trifle second. They pay attention neither to their health nor to their spouse, children or other members in the family. Their days and nights are consumed by one passion—work. All other aspects of life take a back seat. An invisible thread binds them with the hawa-pani of the railways. Wearing the railway uniform is a matter of pride for them. Even if they are suspended, they will not discard their uniform—just as Bholanath had not.

Bholanath considered his duty sacred; his customers—God. As a subordinate employee, he had not taken any customer service training, and he struggled with English. Despite this, his conduct and behaviour with the customers were exemplary, as good as that of any trained executive. When he introduced himself, his smile and warm handshake made for an excellent ice breaker: "I, B.N. Prasad,

Conductor, S.E. Railway. Please come, your berth number is ..."
When the station arrived, he would call the coolie and help unload
the guests' luggage. Such etiquettes and impeccable manners didn't
cost him a penny, and earned him a good name for himself and
his department. For his excellent conduct, he received many awards
from his division and the Railway Board.

Bholanath was not only conscientious but was also blessed
with a towering physique. It was, of course, difficult to tell whether
the members of Railways Service Commission selected him for his
temperament or his impressive physique. Hefty, and at a height of five
feet and eleven inches, he always bagged the role of either *Hanuman*
or *Ravan* in the *Ram Navami* festival of the village or the annual
functions held by the Commercial Department of the division.

In God's creation, physical might and good intentions are
perhaps not matched with equal intelligence. If that was not the case,
the order of creation would have gone a bit awry. Bholanath was
not endowed with a sharp intelligence as much as his good nature
and impressive physique. But that endeared him to all, despite the
difficult circumstances he occasionally found himself in.

Once, a passenger had got down from the compartment, leaving
his umbrella behind. Bholanath got down running behind him,
shouting, "Your umbrella, Sir. Your umbrella." The train chugged
away. Another time, during his wedding procession, the horse he
mounted on got frisky, so Bholanath alighted from the horse and
walked up to the bride's house, while the best boy sat happily on
the horse. The stories about Bholanath had their share of half-truths
and lies. The reason could be that his colleagues were jealous of him,
since he used to bag the prizes. Some of his colleagues were secretly
happy that he was suspended. Though not overtly expressive, on the
sly, they would say, "*Sala!* Was trying to be holier than thou and act
goody-goody. Finally, the sycophant has got his due."

The Senior Divisional Commercial Manager (Sr. DCM) of
Chakradharpur was a lady. Whenever she went for ticket-checking,
Bholanath accompanied him as a bodyguard. The division workers
used to comment that in Chakradharpur, Bholanath was the trusted
Hanuman of *Sita Maiya*. This Sr. DCM was in charge of the enquiry.
She was known to be a tough nut to crack. Bholanath was also not a

person to be intimidated. He knew that madam would have implicit trust in him. But this complaint, he feared, might be a dent on his character.

One incident kept replaying in his mind. During one ticket-checking in the passenger train, Madam was in a tight spot amidst the rice smugglers of Goelkera. The smugglers were up in arms and getting confrontational with the Sr. DCM. Bholanath told her to go to the washroom while he stood guard, showing his back to the smugglers. Kicks and punches rained on his back till Chakradharpur. For him, it was saving his *Sita Maiya*, and he took the assaults sportingly.

Bholanath was on tenterhooks. "What could madam be thinking? Will I be treated like one of those mediocre TTEs? Will Madam treat all the competent, incompetent, inept, proficient, feeble-minded with the same brush?" The thought was so agitating that he had to rush to the tea kiosk every now and then to refresh himself with cups of tea.

***

Sr. DCM Madam was going through the complaints.

The first one read thus:

Sir,

The reason for writing to you is that on 10th of last month, I was travelling in Howrah Ahmedabad Express in AC II tier. I was to go up to Jharsuguda. I had asked the conductor to give me a wakeup call. Because of his negligence, I ended up at Bilaspur. Not only my work was affected, but I also had to incur extra expenditure. When I told him this, he started manhandling me. Such goondaism on the part of a conductor requires proper punishment.

Signed: Kartar Singh

Jamshedpur

PNR No: 611-6610076.

The second complaint was more serious:

Sir,

On the 10th of last month, I was travelling in the Howrah Ahmedabad Express. My reservation was from Howrah to Surat. The conductor and attendant of AC II Tier lifted me like a potato sack and made me get down halfway through my journey. All my pleadings were in vain. I am sure that it was done in order to give somebody a berth. If they are not punished for their demeanour, I shall be forced to write to higher authorities.

Signed: Sartaj Singh

Lindsay Street Kolkata

PNR No: 611-6128310.

Both the complaints had come from Additional General Manager's Complaints cell. The instructions were to immediately suspend the Conductor and send the enquiry report within fifteen days.

The calling bell was heard. The Peon came out and called loudly: "Conductor Bholanath!"

Bholanath abruptly put down his cup of tea and came running. "Yes, I am B.N. Prasad, Conductor"

"Come! Madam is calling you."

Bholanath straightened his coat and tie. He gingerly went inside and stood with his head down.

"What, Bholanath? the railway salary was not enough. You have started eying public money?"

"No, Madam. Please don't think like that. I have not done anything that atrocious."

He then started sobbing. He had not expected such harsh comments.

"I did not expect this from you Bholanath," the Sr. DCM continued.

"Madam, I am innocent. Please listen to my explanation."

"You have brought disrepute to your division. But go on. Tell me what you have to say."

Madam sounded crestfallen, as if she wanted to rebuke him but was not in a position to do so. It made her uncomfortable to have suspended an honest employee like Bholanath.

Bholanath began: "That day, I had started my duty from Chakradharpur station. The train was on time. To my bogie came one Sardarji, who had boarded from Tata Nagar. He told me 'Conductor Sahib, I will be getting down at Jharsuguda station. Please wake me up.' I said, 'Ok I will.' After some time, he came up to me again and said, 'I get deep sleep early in the morning. So please don't forget to wake me up as I have important work.' I made a note of the berth he was in. Then I got busy with my work. I also went to the adjacent first class and supervised it. My duty was up to Bilaspur station. Right before Bilaspur, I was packing my trunk when Sardarji came and caught me by my tie. He said, 'Why didn't you wake me up at Jharsuguda?' I was surprised. I said, 'But I did. I made sure you got down at Jharsuguda station.' Then he started hurling abuses at me. 'You thief, you cheat!' I quietly swallowed all this. I held his hand and said, 'I am sorry.' I even cut him a free EFT from Bilaspur to Jharsuguda. Still, he kept on hurling abuses. Then finally, he said, 'You railway people are all thieves.' This, Madam, I could not take."

"Then what did you do?"

"I balled up all the chart paper I was carrying and stuffed it in his mouth. That was the only way to shut him up."

"Do you think that was the right thing to do, Bholanath? Was that not manhandling?"

"No, Madam. That was not manhandling. I have spent a lifetime in the railways. We know how people are, how to handle each one. So many people board the train. Even if it is written, 'Do not smoke', people do. Consuming alcohol is prohibited on the train, but they still drink. If we ask them not to do so, they abuse us and make complaints about us. Was it not his fault first—to abuse and misbehave with an employee?

Madam did not say anything. After a brief silence, Bholanath said in a low voice, "In the TTE guesthouse, I cried, Madam."

"Why? What happened?"

"In Jharsuguda station, I ran from the first-class compartment to AC II Tier compartment. Woke up Sardarji. He was refusing to get up. I tickled his beard. He looked at me and smiled. I said, 'Sir, get up, please. You have to get down at Jharsuguda.' He sleepily said, 'No, I don't.' The train was about to move. He was not collecting his luggage. I was afraid he would miss his destination. He looked like a helpless innocent child who refuses to wake up. I told the attendant to collect his luggage and get down. I picked him up in my two hands, got down from the train and made him sit on the platform. Then the train left. Only at Bilaspur station, Madam, I realized that I had forced out the wrong Sardarji."

Madam burst out laughing. She laughed so hard that water came out from her eyes and nose. The staff and visitors sitting outside were wondering what was happening behind the doors.

But Bholanath was unperturbed. "Madam, I knew you would laugh. You must think what a stupid fool I am. But please tell me, what else could I have done? I went to the right berth, but I didn't find the Sardarji there. I saw a covered person with two clean feet, and I thought it could not be that of the Sardarji. On the adjacent berth, I saw the head a Sardarji—the wrong one. But he had the same moustache and beard. I thought, 'Perhaps he has slept on the wrong berth by mistake.' And so it was."

Madam again laughed. Not because of Bholanath's foolishness, but for the way he narrated his goof-up.

"Madam, I have committed a grievous mistake. But I did not do it deliberately. Even you would have been deceived."

The Sr. DCM had still not stopped laughing. She rang the bell, and the peon came. "Complaint Inspector!"

Complaint Inspector Mr Banerjee entered.

"Where are the two complainants?"

"They have come, Madam. They are sitting in the ante-room."

"Have they been served tea and biscuit?"

"Yes, Madam"

"What about staying arrangements?"

"A retiring room has been booked, Madam."

"Pass?"

"Pass has been given. Return reservation has also been made, Madam."

"All right. Ask them to come in."

The two men were ushered into the room. The Sr. DCM was astonished to see them. Of the same height and almost similar physique, the two looked twin brothers in a Hindi film. The moustache and beard were also the same. The beard was tied in the same manner. The turbans were the same, except for the colours. It was difficult to tell who was Kartar Singh and who was Sartaj Singh.

Madam told them to sit down. Concealing her amusement, she said, "I am sorry, gentlemen. On behalf of the railways, I seek apologies for the inconvenience caused to you."

"No, Madam. We heard everything. We have also heard about Mr Bholanath and his reputation. We are withdrawing our complaint."

Evergreen

Tearing into the vast Saranda forest extending from Mahadevasal to Manoharpur lies the South Eastern Railway's twin single line. Inside the dense forest falls Posaita, a station that has only a level crossing gate. Through this gate, a red mud road snakes its way into the womb of the forest. On that muddy road sometimes are seen trucks carrying stone chips for the railways. At times are seen trucks laden with stolen timber, plying on the sly under the cover of darkness.

The daytime silence and serenity of the place are broken by the activities in the night. The twinkling stars can hardly be seen from under the dense foliage, but the eyes of the nocturnal animals glow like embers. Cutting through the road, the bear baby rushes to the mahul forest, while the elephants in the herd amble across trampling the bamboo bushes. As the night grows older, tigers are heard growling and owls wailing. As if to keep company, the eagle flaps its wing noisily atop of an arjun tree. To add to the ambience, the nocturnal flowers open up their bottle caps and spray their fragrance into the night sky.

Each night, Sambari, the watchman at the level crossing gate, would get a fright. For twenty years, he had been posted as the gateman and he knows the rulebook of the wild like the back of his hand. Unless their path is obstructed or their food is snatched away from their mouth, the animals do not harm anyone. You stay put in your shack and let them go their way. The motto of the jungle "live and let live" has to be followed in letter and spirit. No one knew this better than Sambari, who had lived alone for twenty years in this tiny shed.

Then again, "alone" would not be the right word. Accompanying Sambari were deities: Bajrangbali, Ganesh, Sita–Ram and Balgopal. Their pictures hung on the unplastered brick wall by the thread of the cobweb. Picture of the forest goddess adorned the outer wall of the hut. Sambari bowed before all the deities, twice every day— once before taking over charge and again while handing over charge to his reliever. His duty was for twelve hours a day, and after every fortnight, his day duty changed to night duty.

One night, during his duty, a jeep stopped near the gate with a spluttering sound. Sambari was jolted out of his half-awake half-asleep stupor. Two officers got down from the jeep. The first officer was a gruff, older man. He had a revolver slung on his shoulder and was wearing gumboots. He looked like a dodgy marksman, and his left eye was a little smaller than the right one. Sambari imagined that aiming the revolver with one eye closed had perhaps resulted in such an asymmetry.

The other officer was a young man. Sambari had seen him during a visit to the division office.

The older officer twirled his moustache and shouted, "Why have you shut the gate?"

Sambari was so perplexed that he forgot his customary *salaam*.

The younger officer said in a low voice, "Bada Sahib has come from the Headquarters."

"In the night, no vehicle can pass this way, Sahib. So I have kept it closed."

"What is written in the working rule of the station?"

"Sahib, whatever may be written in the book, it is safer to keep the gate closed in the night."

At this fearless and unbecoming reply from Sambari, the sahib glared at him with his bulbous eyes, which could frighten an animal.

"I see. The bed is laid. Were you sleeping?'

"My reliever has not come, Sahib. So I was lying down."

"The gate is closed. But why is your red light switched off?"

Before Sambari could reply, the young officer interjected. "Perhaps it has been put off by the wind, Sir."

The bulging eyes now focused on the young officer. "You are very strange, Mister. How will you control the staff? Are you protecting them?"

The young officer kept quiet.

"Why are you quiet? Check the records of the gate. See if all the equipment is in good condition. Check the private number."

The young officer had been posted to Chakradharpur division as Divisional Operating Superintendent (DOS) only a year back. The sahib's commanding tone made him nervous, and he started dialling the magneto phone. He checked whatever numbers had been exchanged with the nearby stations.

Red and green flags, hand signal lamp, banner flag, detonator box with one dozen detonators—all the safety equipment was in order.

"Everything is okay, Sir."

"Test his safety knowledge."

The young DOS then asked Sambari what to do if the gate was broken; at what distance to place the detonator in case of a train accident; where to put the banner flag; and when to exchange the private number. Sambari had an experience of twenty years. All the steps and measures of safety were at his fingertips. He had prevented many accidents by detecting hotbox of a goods train, hanging rods and flat tyres. For such timely detections, he had been decorated with awards from the DRM and the GM. Naturally, he was fearless before the examiners and was even smiling to himself.

But the older officer's eyes were burning like flashbulbs; he found Sambari's confidence impertinent. "Open the gate," he said.

Anxious, Sambari opened the gate slowly. Taking big strides, the sahib advanced towards the jeep. While crossing the gate to enter into Saranda jungle, he glared at Sambari for the last time. Sambari blew his whistle to give the all-clear signal, which was perhaps like a blow to the officer's ego.

Once in the vehicle, he gave instructions to the young officer. "Suspend the Gateman."

"But, Sir … He is a sincere worker!"

"He was asleep during duty hours. What sincerity?"

"Sir, there is no traffic at this gate at night. Further, it is much safer to keep the gate closed."

The older officer growled, "Will you take action, or do I have to take action against you?" then, turning away he muttered to himself, "Does not know how to behave. Questioning me … arrogant bugger!" Throughout the ride, he kept mumbling angrily. His mood was worsened by the sheer lack of deer or fowl in the whole of Saranda jungle.

The young DOS, in the back seat, could do nothing but sit in quiet fright, wondering at the whims of his egocentric boss and his equally futile hunting expedition.

***

Sambari was suspended from his job. As per rules, an enquiry was conducted. At the time of enquiry, he did not contest the fact of his lying down while on duty and having closed the gate. He gave a true account of his conduct. His past record of having received two awards and the appreciations from his supervisors could not save him. The young DOS was fraught with guilt, as he had to sign the documents that gave the orders for Sambari's dismissal.

Strict orders were issued from the department. No compromise on safety. Any deviation would attract zero tolerance. Severe punishments on a few would send the right signal to all and act as a deterrent for the other employees, especially in matters of safety. And that is how the enquiry was summed up.

Sambari's supervisors asked him to appeal to the higher authorities against the dismissal. Sambari did so, but the senior officer,

Misra Sahib, to whom DOS reported, upheld the punishment. He did not want to create a storm in the teacup in the Headquarters.

***

Three years passed. The young DOS, Siddharth, was still working in the division, buried in work. At times, he was rankled by Sambari's thoughts—more so while travelling in the air-conditioned coupe through the Posaita level crossing gate. The sound of the all-clear whistle at the gate used to remind him of Sambari's intrepid and plucky attitude and his own helplessness in the entire episode concerning his dismissal.

***

Twelve years later, Siddharth found himself in a plum posting, as the Chairman of the Railway Recruitment Board. Hundreds of candidates were hired under his orders. A drive was on for filling up the vacant posts earmarked for scheduled caste and scheduled tribes, as per the directives of the central government. The Chairman was directed to tour the tribal areas to search for suitable candidates, since issuing notifications and advertisements in newspapers did not garner adequate candidates for the unfilled vacancies. Inspired by such a proactive directive, the Chairman was often seen touring the tribal districts of Phulbani, Kalahandi, Keonjhar, Singhbhum, and Ranchi.

Siddharth kept his tour programme at Singhbhum district. He had in mind to meet his old colleagues and employees of Chakradharpur Division. Another secret agenda was to trace the whereabouts of Sambari, who had been rendered jobless fifteen years ago. *What would he be doing?* Age would have bent his back. His hair would have turned white, like the jute grass. How had his poor family sustained itself? Could he do something for him and atone for the sin committed fifteen years back?

Getting down from Utkal Express at Manoharpur, Chairman Siddharth took a jeep towards the level crossing gate. From there, his jeep raced on a narrow road to reach the village of Sambari. On both sides was the tranquil Saranda jungle. The green cover of sal and shisham trees stood in contrast to the yellow dress worn by mahul and asan trees. The gulmohar and shimli trees were a riot of reds.

Even the humble grass was sporting its flower stalks, as if to compete with the flowering trees. A treasure trove of fragrance—as if saved over the years—was sweeping the forest. Siddharth was soaking in the aroma and the untamed silence of the forest while imagining himself to be a godsend for the area.

After an hour of bumpy drive on the muddy road full of potholes, he reached Sambari's village. Two rows of huts facing each other on the foothills of a small hillock stared at him. In the not-so-far hillock were carved out parcels of cultivated land, of oilseeds, perhaps. At places near the village, goats and sheep were grazing.

But Siddharth could not focus on any of this. In his mind, he imagined a warm welcome from Sambari—for coming to his aid. *I will bring back the smile to his face after fifteen years,* Siddharth thought.

Seeing the jeep on the village road, a few piglets went helter-skelter. Behind them were running a few semi-clad kids. Sambari was not at home. So Siddharth had to sit on the cot in front of his house and wait for him.

When Sambari finally arrived, at first, he could not recognize Siddharth. How could he? The thick mop of black hair of his youth had given way to a few strands of hair on his forehead as a reminder of the past. Sambari, however, was looking the same, like an evergreen forest tree.

"Sambari! Do you recognize me? I was the DOS of Chakradharpur?"

Sambari nodded.

"So how are you Sambari?"

"I am fine, Sahib."

His short reply sounded like a throwaway sentence. It did not have a trace of earnestness.

"How are you managing, Sambari?"

"Managing okay, Sahib. Both good and bad. This jungle,

mountain and spring are our father and mother." Then he fell silent.

Siddharth felt that in this single sentence, he had summarized the essence of his life. "Sambari, the railways had not done justice to you. I have come today to make amends. My order took away your job. If you have any son or daughter, today, I can give them jobs."

There was no reaction on Sambari's face. His silence transported Siddharth to the scene where hundreds lined up in front of his office and home daily for a coveted job in the Indian Railways. Ministers and high-ranking officials send recommendations on a daily basis for their protégé for a job, and he finds it difficult to accommodate them all. Here, Sambari was silent. *What has happened to him? Has he become averse to the railways due to his past experience?*

He pushed a paper form into his hand and said;

"Sambari! Fill up this application form."

A faint smile crossed Sambari's face. "But Sahib, I don't have any children."

On the ride back through the jungle, Siddharth felt listless. He felt as if he had invaded the jungle—like an unwanted cloud with unseasonal rain.

Ghost of Bhanwartonk

The king is worshipped in his own country, while the learned are worshipped everywhere … so had said Chanakya. But the latter part of the adage has no meaning these days. To say only film people and cricketers are worshipped will be closer to the truth.

While travelling in Bhubaneswar-LTT Express, this writer, who considers himself a learned man, realized the absurdity of the adage.

That day, a film producer and a film director arriving last minute at the station had created quite a flutter. To bid them goodbye, a big bunch of admirers had descended on the platform. It transpired that the duo was scheduled to fly to Mumbai. But due to the cancellation of the flight and their urgency to reach Mumbai, they were forced to travel by train.

Seeing them, the conductor who is always used to giving stock negatives—"no room ... No room"—became a magician, conjuring up two berths in AC II Tier from his bag of tricks and ushering them to their seats.

I had a lower berth in the same compartment where they were allotted the two berths. The conductor recognized me and introduced the two visitors to me. "Sir, this is Mr Gadadhar Champatiray, well-known film producer; and he is Mr Kunmun Mohanty, film director."

The conductor did not forget to introduce me to them either. "He is our Retired CCM—Chief Commercial Manager. A big writer." Then, in the same self-effacing pose, he continued, "Sir! I could give only one lower and one upper berth. There is a rush on the train today. Please don't mind, Sir!"

"It is okay …" With innate ease, the two gentlemen settled in the berth opposite mine.

I was meeting these two veterans of the Odia film world for the first time. Like people inhabiting two unknown continents, we greeted each other with synthetic smiles.

I had read about these two big names from the newspapers. The producer was implicated in a case of real-estate fraud and had been to jail. The director had a casting couch allegation against him.

***

After the train started, some passengers came to meet the two and made polite enquiries. Among the callers were good-looking females. For some time, the compartment saw a spate of visitors. Needless to say, I was not attracting even a side glance. I felt that I was being denied the customary formal conversation with them.

Here, I had about thirty Odia story collections and novels to my credit, but not a single story had had the fortune of being translated into celluloid. So remorse was always simmering within me. Now, seeing these two veterans in person, my long-suppressed desire was rekindled. I thought of asking them to film one of my stories.

The very next moment, however, my conscience stopped me. This was my first meeting with them. Moreover, their persona was somehow not eliciting any feelings of respect in me. The producer looked like a well-fed wild buffalo and the director was like a cunning fox.

After a long Hamletian dilemma—To? Or not to?—I decided I ought to. *Their fortunes are high … they are at the pinnacle.* In order to achieve one's objective, an intelligent person has to ignore one's principles, values, and ego hassles. Even Lord Krishna had to touch a donkey's feet.

To win their hearts and minds, I had to get an opportunity. The pantry car attendant appeared on the scene to take the order for breakfast and lunch. I told the bearer, "We are all travelling together. Go and call the Manager. Tell him that in berth number 15, CCM Sir is travelling. Ask him to come and meet me. We will place the orders when he comes."

The manager came running in no time, with his coat buttoned wrong. In a supplicant mood, he said, "Sir, Namaskar. Please give me a chance to serve you."

I introduced the two celebrity gentlemen and said, "They are my guests. Breakfast, lunch—everything should be special. You understand? The cheque is on me."

The manager replied, "You must not pay, Sir! It is our pleasure. I will see to it that only the best is served. The choicest in veg and non-veg will come to you, Sir!"

"Okay. First send special tea in the flasks."

Having seen this interaction unfold, one of the two gentlemen ventured, "You have retired, I suppose?"

With a puffed-up heart, I said, "Yes, the elephant is worth a lakh when alive and also when dead."

Both of them gave a wry smile, but it sparked a conversation between us. We spoke of random things, like the weather, the newly formed Modi government, and other odd issues. After being treated to the royal breakfast and special tea, the two warmed up further. We started to chat like thick friends.

The director asked, "How many books have you written?"

Promptly, I replied, "Thirty!"

"Then you must have built a mansion, like Bibhuti Babu."

I smiled and said, "To publish my books, I had to sell my Housing Board Flat in Sambar Patia of Dhenkanal."

"How come?"

"That is a long story. But to cut it short, one of my books was selected for Operation Blackboard. We had orders to print seven hundred books. But due to a court injunction, the state government refused to take our books. They became food for the termites. I had to bear a loss of forty thousand rupees in those days—the 90s. I had to sell the Dhenkanal flat to pay the printing press people." Then, to get their sympathy, I added, "I will show you the house from the rail track." I breathed a sigh.

When the train crossed Garh Dhenkanal, with sad eyes, I looked at my erstwhile dwelling. I could not get an opportunity to show it to the gentlemen, however. The producer had gone to the washroom and the director was making rings of smoke with eyes closed. He had offered me a fag, but I had politely declined.

"Smoking is Not Permitted" was written large over berth 17. Somehow, I was consciously putting up with such a defiant attitude. The occupant on the berth above me was a young person who was blissfully under the spell of sleep. After the smoke session was over, the conversation turned towards Odia cinema.

"What is your opinion about Odia cinema?' the director asked.

If it was someone else, I would have replied in one word: "Rubbish." But I regained my composure and said, "After staying long years in cities outside of Odisha, I have just come back to Bhubaneswar. I have not seen many Odia films of late. One thing I have noticed is that films are not being made on classic novels, as was done earlier. Like *Mala Janha, Kaa,* and *Chhaman Atha Gunth.* Why is it so?"

The director replied, almost apologetically, "We make films to cater to the audience. If we make films on classics, the producers will have to sell *their* houses. Besides, where are the good stories in Odia?"

This was my opportunity to put forth my proposal. "I have a good story. Will you listen? If you make a film on the story, I will not charge you anything. I just need a name."

The special breakfast and tea had done the trick. They now seemed amicable towards me. Not just that, I had even offered my lower berth to them and volunteered to take the upper berth. The director looked at my white mop of hair and said, "You are a retired senior citizen. Will it not inconvenience you to take the upper berth?"

I said, "We are railway people. We are used to travelling in the engine footplate or the guard's brake van. Roughing it out in train journeys has become a part of our being. And are you surprised seeing this white hair? Hasn't the poet said, "They are not old whose hair has become white'?"

We all laughed at the joke. The young man on the upper berth joined us in our laughter.

I reiterated, "Shall I recount you the freshly minted story of mine? Mind you, this is a true railway story."

"Railway story? That must be interesting. Okay tell us," said the director.

And so I began …

(2)

That was a quivering wintery morning. The sky was innocently blue. Wispy clouds were floating across the sky like white swans.

The Bilaspur controller called the Station Master of Khongsara.

"Hello, Khongsara?"

"Yes, Khongsara."

"Give clearance to I-Sakurbasti coal train."

"Ok."

The Khongsara Station Master rang out a *tong-tong* sound to signal for line clearance from Bhanwartonk station. When the line clear permission was given by the Station Master of Bhanwartonk, a token came out of the block instrument. Handing the token to the porter, the Station Master said, "I-Sakurbasti goods will pass. Tie it well with the hoop and give the token to the driver." Then, he instructed the cabin men of east cabin and west cabin to lower the signal after setting the mainline. Both obeyed and gave private numbers. The I-Sakurbasti train crossed the Khongsara station at 8 a.m. The two cabin men of east and west, showed the green flag and exchanged signals with the driver and the guard.

Till that point, all was well. The running time between Khongsara and Bhanwartonk was twenty-five minutes. But even after a passage of fifty minutes, the train had not reached Bhanwartonk. Since it was an interchange train, the controller was keeping an eye on its movement and had instructed a few stations ahead to give it a through-pass signal.

Not having received the out-report from Bhanwartonk, the agitated controller said, "Hello Bhanwartonk?"

"Yes, Bhanwartonk."

"When did Khongsara give the out report?"

"At 8."

"Then where did the train go?"

"How to say? This is a hilly terrain. Might have run into some problem."

"Heard any whistle?"

"No."

"Any call from the emergency phone?"

"No."

Those days—the early 80s of the last century—guards and drivers had no phones. Some telephone poles had emergency sockets. But most of the time, they did not work. The Khongsara–Bhanwartonk section was situated in a wildlife infested area, so guards and drivers hesitated to go on foot to the phone.

After the passage of one hour, a "jham-jham" beating sound was heard on the track. The Bhanwartonk Station Master and the porter raised their ears. Eventually, the diesel engine of the train crossed the station at a high speed. Nobody took the token from the hands of the porter nor was a signal exchanged with the station.

"Boss, the train has not come. The engine is running, just like a wild buffalo runs after breaking his bridle. Nobody took the token from me."

The Station Master was petrified. He screamed into the control phone, "Hello, control Bhanwartonk!"

"Yes, Bhanwartonk."

"Only the light engine passed. Nobody took the line clear token."

"Is anybody there in the engine?"

"I did not see anybody. Nobody exchanged the signal." He added, "The engine is running at a speed of a hundred kilometres."

"Something has gone terribly wrong. If the engine has no driver or assistant … is a ghost driving it?" The controller then informed the CHC, Subba Rao.

Years of experience sat easily on the shoulders of Rao. He called the station ahead, "Hello, Khodri?"

"Yes, Khodri."

"Chief Controller speaking. Now at 9.10, one diesel light engine has passed Bhanwartonk. Looks unmanned. Cancel the line clear. Immediately set the catch siding line. In the station ahead is standing Utkal Express. Otherwise, a disaster will happen."

"Okay, Sir." Cancelling the line clear, the Khodri Station Master instructed the west cabin man, "Set the catch siding line … fast!"

The three stations of Khongsara, Bhanwartonk, and Khodri and the control room were thrown into turmoil, while the commotion spread to all the stations upon overhearing the conversations on the control line. Even with the knowledge of impending disaster, the Khodri Station Master, counting days for his retirement, started reciting the Hanuman Chalisa, hoping that a miracle would happen.

The Khongsara–Bhanwartonk and Khodri section is the most eventful one in Bilaspur division. Every day, some event or the other takes place there. In 1981, a dreadful accident of a passenger train had claimed the lives of almost forty people. Derailment at regular intervals is also a common occurrence. Sometimes, elephant herds block the train; at other times, ferocious tigers get seated like emperors inside the tunnels. Many rail employees have lost their lives to the wild animals. While crossing the section not only the rail employees but also the passengers remember their Gods. People say that the ghosts of all those who have lost their lives unnaturally roam the section, and the frequent accidents are the doings of these ghosts.

The Senior Divisional Operations Operating Superintendent (Sr. DOS) and other officers rushed to the Control office. A siren was blown in Bilaspur. A long one, and that too five times. When the news of an accident is heard, this heart-rending siren is blown so that the officers and staff of the relief train can prepare to go to the accident site. As the Safety Officer of the Division, I set out with my line box.

The accident had happened at Khodri station. The runaway engine entered the catch siding, shattered the dead-end, and plunged into the nearby Malania river.

There was no trace of the driver and the assistant driver. I-Sakurbasti goods train had thirty box wagons. To trace the wagons, the banking-engine was sent from Khongsara station to mid-section.

Waiting for the train, the exhausted Guard Harinarayan had fallen asleep. When the banking engine dragged the wagons, he woke up from his sleep and started asking, "Why are you pulling it back? If the train is not able to move because of the upward gradient, then give the train a push."

"Guard Babu, your train has met with an accident. It has fallen into the river with its outstretched limbs. And you are snoring here?"

"What accident?" He took out his leather pouch and downed all the water.

After the goods train was pulled back to Khongsara station, the relief train rushed towards Khodri. Along with other officers, I was also present in the relief train. Reaching Khodri, we had a view of the gruesome spectacle of the accident. The barricade at the dead-end was smashed into smithereens, and the diesel engine had sunk into the overflowing river. The possibility of retrieving the engine from the river with the help of a crane also looked remote.

"Gone … ten lakhs down the drain!" lamented the Divisional

Mechanical Engineer (Carriage & Wagon).

"Rebuilding the track and the dead end will be a tough job," the Divisional Civil Engineer chimed in.

As a Safety Officer, running to all the accident sites was my primary duty. After reaching the place, I made a sketch of the accident site and reported the loss and destruction to the Headquarters. Regarding the driver and the assistant, many onlookers said that they had likely met their watery grave. So, it did not strike anyone to search for their bodies using a boat.

After going to the station, I started my investigation. I asked the cabin-man of the East Cabin, "Did you see anyone in the engine?"

He trembled and answered, "Yes, sir. A dark-looking man was seen sitting there."

"Driver Radheshyam and Assistant Natharam … neither of them is dark. Whom did you see?"

"Don't know, Sir. Perhaps a ghost!"

The cabin-man of the West Cabin said, "The engine shot past in the blink of an eye, raising a dust storm. In that cloud of dust, Sir, I could see nothing."

The token porter said, "I was standing at the side of the track, holding the token. Nobody was in the engine."

The Station Master said, "I was standing with the green flag in the platform. Nobody exchanged the signal."

How the train engine got detached from the rake and what happened to the driver and his assistant remained a mystery.

***

The young man sleeping on the upper berth came down and asked, "Uncle was anything unearthed after that?'

The producer and director were also curious. "Were whereabouts of the driver and the assistant discovered?"

Chai … Chai … coffee … coffee!

The call from the hawker was heard along the corridor. I took a break from my storytelling and ordered four cups of coffee.

After two swigs of coffee, I started the story again.

***

As per the procedure, a formal enquiry was set up. As a DSO, I was a member of the team. The other two members were the Sr. DME (Carriage and Wagon) and the DME (Power). Due to the breakage of the coupling between the engine and the first wagon, the engine got detached, and because it was at top speed, the engine hurtled down and met with an accident. Till this point, we were of the same opinion. But who is responsible for such a thing? On this issue, both the officers blamed each other.

The Sr. DME said, "Because of over-speeding by the driver, the coupling got broken."

The DME (P) remarked, "Bilaspur Yard has been selected for making an intensive examination point of the wagons. Your staff did not check the couplings properly. So they are responsible."

On this issue, both the officers almost came to blows. I pacified them with tea and biscuits. Finally, we came to the conclusion that due to absence of primary witnesses, it is difficult to pinpoint and arrive at the exact reason for the accident. We submitted a report on these lines to the DRM.

Though I was a favourite of the DRM, Saxena Sahib, he admonished me saying, "The other two officers have reported in a manner to save their departments. But being neutral, why did you agree to it? This is a Board case. The Board will never agree." Then, he gave his verdict like King Solomon: "The two departments are responsible—50 percent each."

Whatever may be the verdict of the enquiry report, in the common man's Mindspace, the event remained as a "ghost-driven" accident.

After this, I was transferred from Bilaspur to Chakradharpur and lost track of the later events.

[3]

Twenty-five years later, the mystery of the incident came to my knowledge when I was posted for the second time as CCM at Bilaspur. The truth never remains hidden. One day, it comes to the light. Now here is how the accident had actually happened.

***

That day, after crossing the station Khongsara, the wheels of the train slipped in the ghat section of the jungle. The wheels of the engine rotated and could not pull the train ahead.

Natharam said, "Master, open the sander."

"I have done it," replied Radheshyam.

"Increase the notch."

"Have done it. Why is the engine not moving still? Nathu, go down and see."

Natharam came down from the engine and saw that the sand is exhausted from the sander. Some unknown leaves had fallen on the tracks, making it oily, and that's why the train had stalled.

Hearing this, Radheshyam instructed, "Throw ballasts under the wheels."

"Okay, master." He went on putting ballasts under the wheels … but it did not yield any result.

"Wait, let me come down," said Radheshyam. He went down and also started putting ballasts under the wheels. Now both of them walked beside the two sides, putting ballasts under the wheels. The train started to move a little …

Then, all of a sudden, the engine detached itself from the rake and started moving at lightning speed. Both Radheshyam and Natharam were left behind while the engine sped away. Petrified at the sudden movement, they sat down with hands on their heads.

"Master, what shall we do now?'

"I have no idea. We will be severely punished. One of us should have stayed in the engine. The department will make examples out of us. We will lose our jobs. Or worse—prison!"

"So, what do we do?"

"Let us go into the jungle and think."

The two men vanished into the Achanakmar jungle. Achanakmar is a dense forest in the Vindhya mountain range. It is devoid of human habitation and has been declared a sanctuary for its variety of wildlife. Radheshyam and Natharam risked their lives in that jungle for a few days and then somehow escaped to Mathura and Vrindavan.

Their families were devastated. The wives had to go through the rituals of breaking their bangles and wiping the vermillion from their foreheads. I, the DPO (Divisional Personnel Officer), and the DME, were deputed by the DRM to the families to convey our condolences. The DPO assured family pension for both the families and compassionate appointment for the Radheshyam's son and Natharam's wife.

The files of Radheshyam and Natharam moved speedily in the corridors of railway administration unlike the normal TA, OT bills, pension etc, where greasing the palm of the lower-level functionaries is a common and accepted practice. Only in the case of unnatural deaths are such hurdles not raised.

After a few months, I discovered Radheshyam's son, Kanheya, in the yard, working as an engine khalasi and Natharam's wife, Kamali, as an ayah in the ladies waiting room.

By the time Radheshyam and Natharam, with overgrown beards and matted locks, came back to Bilaspur in disguise to find out about their families, their worlds had turned upside down. Radheshyam's wife—with his son, daughter-in-law, and grandson—was leading a full life. Natharam's wife had been forcibly married off to his younger brother-in-law.

The two men did not think it appropriate to stay in Bilaspur, which would invite trouble for their families. During that time, a bunch of sadhus were going to Amarkantak. Natharam said, "Master, let us go to Amarkantak."

"Yes, there is no other way out. Let us go."

So, chanting "Narmada Maia ki jai", they joined the sadhus.

***

After many years, a huge mela was put up in Amarkantak. A fifty-member party on a bus from Bilaspur had gone to visit the mela. Radheshyam's son, Kanheya, was the organizer. His mother and sister, and Natharam's wife and daughter had joined the party.

While resting in a temple premises, Radheshyam's wife happened to see two bearded sadhus with matted locks under a banyan tree. She called her son and asked, "Babu re ... those two sadhus look familiar. Will you go and ask them where they are from?"

Kanheya went and paid obeisance to the two sadhus. "Where have you come from?" he asked.

Radheshyam replied, "Baba, where are you from? We are Aghoris. The world is our home."

But it did not take much time for Kanheya to remove the veil of secrecy. "Father, my eyes do not cheat me. You are my father, and he is Natharam Uncle!" Then, he fell before their feet and wept inconsolably. "Father, where did you disappear? We thought you had died."

Radheshyam narrated the entire story. Then he said, "Babu re ... keep the mystery a secret. Otherwise, a huge upheaval will surface. Both your job and Kamali's job will be terminated. They will also stop the family pension. What is good for the maximum number of people is the most desirable thing to do."

"No, father, you must come back," Kanheya insisted.

"Don't insist Babu … all the roads are closed for us. Natharam's situation is even more delicate. With what face will Kamali meet him?"

Natharam, with tears in his eyes, said, "Kamali will not come near me. But I want to see my daughter once."

Radheshyam told Kanheya, "When the rest of the guests are at the sit-down feast in the temple premises, you come with your mother and Kamali. Now go, don't crowd this place."

At the appointed time, Kanheya went with his mother and Kamali. The two women were speechless. Tears ran down their cheeks. Natharam put his hand on his daughter Muniya's head, which frightened her, thinking the sadhu is a child snatcher.

Kamali pulled her pallu and stood motionless. Radheshyam's wife said, "Why did you make everyone suffer, while also suffering yourself?"

"It's all destiny," said Radheshyam.

The fully veiled Kamali said, sobbing, "Please don't mind my mistake, Muniya's father!"

"What is your mistake? It is all up to fate," replied Natharam.

Groups of devotees were milling around crossing the road. The secretive meeting had to end.

Radheshyam told his son, "Babu, your mother is under your care now. Maina has come with you, na? Give her hand to a good boy. Also look after Natharam's daughter. You leave us to our karma."

"Father, why do you say that? You were only trying to save the train from stalling. What was your mistake?"

"Remember Babu, one day you may become a driver. In the railway rule book, it is written that driver and the assistant should never leave the engine at the same time. Because of our mistake, this tragedy happened! Remember these simple rules. Now go."

Finally, Natharam told his wife, "Never tell Muniya that her father was a fugitive."

By the time the Bilaspur party wrapped up their trip, Radheshyam and Natharam had vanished from the place.

[4]

My young co-passenger's eyes were moist. He asked, "what steps did the railway take after the story was unravelled?"

"By the time I had gone there, in my second stint, the history and geography of the place had changed considerably," I said. "Bilaspur division had been taken out of South Eastern Railway and merged with South East Central Railway. Old files and records had been consigned to the dustbin. Radheshyam, Natharam, and the strange accident had become part of folklore. Old officers were no longer around. Who would take action and against whom?"

The directed commented, "Interesting!"

"Touching story," added the producer.

By that time, our special lunch had been served. I was feeling elated that my story had touched a chord in the hearts of the listeners. I ordered one more lunch for the young man and invited him to join us. He accepted without a word.

After lunch, the producer and director thanked me for my hospitality.

"If you have liked my story, then make a film on it. I am prepared to write the script. I will not take a penny for the story or for the script."

Seeing them silent, I added, "A film requires every shade of emotion: tragedy, comedy, mystery, suspense, variety ... and a message. My story has all the elements."

The producer and the director—makers of Odia films *Balunga Toka, Udandi Toki, Danthada Neta*—looked at each other.

The director said, "Please don't mind, but in our state, such a film will not work."

The producer added, "It has no sex, no violence, no fighting scene. Not even a song and dance routine."

I remained silent. The jury was out. Without any mistake, the accused was being punished. For the remaining time of the journey, I slept on the upper berth.

[4]

I reached Navi Mumbai in the afternoon and went to my son's place, where my wife was staying. Seeing my deflated face, my wife asked, "what happened? Why do you look dejected?"

Don't disclose defeats, so say the wise. So I kept quiet.

But in the evening, while having tea, I narrated the entire story to my wife. The wise have also said not to keep any secret from your life partner.

My wife never leaves an opportunity to tease me. She said, "Why were you so hospitable to the two ghosts? You are also one ghost. So what else will you do?"

[5]

After some days, the young co-passenger from the eventful train journey unexpectedly landed at our Navi Mumbai address.

"Sir, I am working as an assistant to Vishal Bharadwaj. You must have seen his films like *Omkara, Saat Khoon Maaf* ... made on unusual themes. One day, I narrated your story to him. He said he would like to make a film on this and has sent me to you. Not only that, he intends to give you the role of DRM, Shri Saxena Sahib. Like he had given Ruskin Bond a small role in *Saat Khoon Maaf*, to honour him."

I was flummoxed.

"*Kaloyam nirabadhi, bipula cha prithvi* (Huge is the world, inexorable is the march of time)."

This adage was ringing in my ears, and it felt as if my feet were not touching the floor.

I found myself telling my wife, "Hold me."

Nirbhaya

Kring! Kring! The control phone in the cabin rang out incessantly. Pawan Kumar could hear the long tone as he took rapid strides towards his room after exchanging the signal of the Down Shalimar Goods Train. He rushed to pick up the phone; all the while cursing his job in this godforsaken station.

Pawan Kumar was the ASM of Bhalulata station, at the outskirts of the Saranda forest. The station was indeed godforsaken. Neither a human settlement nor a market had ever sprung up during its long existence; not a ghost of a chance for any entertainment either. Two years into his marriage, Pawan Kumar hadn't yet felt confident enough to bring his wife, Muniya, where he had been posted, which only added to the young man's agony.

Picking up the phone, he replied, "Hello, Bhalu speaking."

From the other end came the Section Controller's yell. "Hello, Bhalu?"

"Yes, Bhalu."

"Where did you vanish to, Pawan?"

"Where will I vanish, Sir? I was passing the Down Shalimar, Sir."

"Why didn't you send the porter for the signal exchange?"

"The porter will be on the off-side. Don't I have to be at the station platform, Sir? Have you forgotten the lessons of Sini Training

School, Sir?" Pawan Kumar was getting brusque.

"Okay, okay. Don't try to teach me. Mumbai–Howrah Mail has left Rourkela. The grant line is clear."

There was no stoppage for the Mumbai–Howrah Mail at Bhalulata station. A through pass had to be given from the mainline. So he put down the phone and dialled the Magneto phone that was connected to the switchman in the West cabin.

There was no response from the West cabin. He kept on dialling the Magneto phone again and again, which only resounded with gurgling sounds and no response. In an agitated voice, he asked the porter who had come back to the station, "Where is that idiot Govardhan?"

Tikra, the porter replied, "I don't know, Chotta Sahib."

"What? It's not yet 6 in the evening," he barked. "Has he drunk mahuli and gone to sleep or what?"

Tikra brought down the hand signal lamp from the lamp room, then said, "Sahib, I am putting on the hand lamp."

Meanwhile, calls started to come in from the Control Room.

"Hello! Hello, Bhalu! Why are you not granting a line clear?"

"Telling the West cabin to do so," he said. "Hey, Tikra! Go and see where that stupid Govardhan is? Is he dead or alive?"

Carrying the hand signal, Tikra set off for the West cabin.

Bhalulata station had neither a good shed nor a parcel office. Only two rooms made up the station. One was the Station Master's room and the other was the ASM's. Adjacent to that was an asbestos roofed second class waiting hall. A small partition separated the waiting hall and the ASM's room. From the window, tickets were sold, above which was displayed a signboard that read "Booking office". In the daytime, the Station Master carried out that duty. In two other two, two ASMs performed the job. In each shift, there were one porter and two switchmen.

On both sides of the station lay a thick sal forest. Even during the day, the station appeared deserted, with an emptiness that gnawed. For the employees of the station, life was tough. One year ago, Maoists had attacked the station and kidnapped three employees.

Pawan Kumar apprehended danger. How had such a thing happened?

Govardhan, the switchman, had come for duty at four in the afternoon. Before coming in for work, he had eaten a sumptuous feast in the basti, which was a good reason for his bowels to work overtime. After granting the line clear to the Down Shalimar Goods Train, he had rushed to attend to nature's call, keeping the hand signal aside on the windowsill. The cabin had no provisions for a toilet, so the workmen had to traverse the jungle nearby. Downstairs from the cabin was the battery room. The room was opened only when the signal department's workmen visited. The points and signal levers jutted out of the roof of the battery room, much like spears. Besides the levers, the room had one table, on which was kept the block instrument, a stool to sit on and an earthen pitcher with drinking water in it. From a distance, the decrepit cabin looked like the room of a departed soul and the hand signal lamp on the windowsill, like the eye of a ghost.

The Magneto phone rang incessantly. Govardhan was barely able to get up until nature's job was finished with. Then he had to clean himself with water from the lota. Rushing through his ablutions in that mildly chilly evening, he was about to climb the stairs up to the cabin, when he saw something that made him freeze. He was barely able to steady himself at the bottom of the steps. Where would he go? By sheer instinct, he climbed up the banyan tree that canopied atop the cabin.

Mumbai–Howrah Mail had stopped near Bisra station. The Controller was like a storm. "The mail is being detained, Pawan Kumar! You will lose your job."

"Sir! What can I do? The switchman is not in the cabin."

"Where has he gone?"

"I don't know, Sir. He is not picking up the phone. I have sent the porter."

Pawan Kumar was at his wits" end. He was musing, "Why me? Why do I get such a posting and have to die every day?"

Tikra was approaching the West cabin with the hand signal lamp swivelling in his hands, with a tune on his lips. In that semi-darkness, the yellow light of the lamp reflected on to his violet-coloured shorts, which hung loose on his curved and rickety legs. He almost looked like a headless phantom.

Coming close to the cabin, he yelled, "Govardhan kaka … Govardhan kaka!"

He was startled when the response to his yell was a whistle that came from the treetop nearby. Reflexively, he spat upon his chest. Then he heard Govardhan's whisper. "Shh … Shhh … Don't go there … shh. Bears … two of them.

Tikra looked here and there, up and down into the cabin and what he saw inside made the lamp drop from his hand. Finding no other escape, he too climbed up the banyan tree.

Now, the two of them, both holding on to dear life on two different branches of the same tree started to whisper to each other. Govardhan hissed, "Not one bhai, there are two of them. I saw one hanging on to the lever handle. Tikra whispered back, "but how did they enter the cabin? Did you keep the mahuli vessel there?"

"*Na re baba, na* … After they have tightened the safety drills, I am one to bring my malpani to the cabin. Don't I love my job?"

"Now tell me what we should do. There the mail train is stuck. Chhota Sahib is restless. Our jobs may go."

"Let the train remain standing. Who cares? We have to survive fast. If we die, will the Railways give back our life? Now look, look … one of the bears is coming down. Let the night pass. Let the other one come down too."

"You remember that person in our basti whose nose was pulled up to his forehead by a bear?"

"Ya ... I remember his disfigured face; his eye was dangling near his mouth thanks to the bear's attack. How ravenous these animals are!"

Meanwhile, seconds and minutes were ticking by. Fifteen minutes must have passed. No sign of Tikra. Pawan Kumar was pacing up and down inside his room. Each minute felt like an hour for him. He sensed that something horrendous had happened.

"Hello, Control ... Bhalu speaking. Bhattacharya Babu! I think some disaster has happened. Both Govardhan and Tikra have vanished." His voice was so nervous, he was unable to say anything more.

"Where is your Bada babu?"

"He has gone to Rourkela, Sir. His family stays there."

Section Controller got irritated and went to the CHC chamber.

A bewildered Pawan Kumar sat down to ruminate; his head clasped in his hands and his elbows on the table. Muniya had been adamant that she would come with him to Bhalulata. He had comforted her, saying that he would bring her with him once was posted to a better station. Every fifteen minutes a train passes through Bhalulata, and taking a leave was a difficult sum to crack. Lack of relieving staff. That was the usual response of the Divisional Traffic Inspector (DTI). "What about the overtime you are earning, Mister?" used to be his own snide remark to them. Muniya, unaware about the goings-on in a mammoth organization like the railways, had to keep her mouth shut and she had shed silent tears.

Meanwhile, a commotion had erupted in Bisra and the other stations where the trains had been detained. The Control Room in Chakradharpur was on edge. DyCHC, CHC, AOS—they all reached the Section Control cabin. Section Controller announced, "Switchman of Bhalu station has absconded. Mumbai–Howrah mail is detained in Bisra and is waiting for a signal from Bhalu station."

"Bhalu station?"

The newly joined AOS was not used to the coded language of the Section Controller.

"Sir, Bhalu is the short form of Bhalulata station."

"Oh, I see! Suspend the switchman."

"But, Sir … the entire station is in a mode of suspension," said the Section Controller. "Both the switchman and the porter have fled, Sir! Please have a look at the chart. The entire movement of trains has come to a dead halt. All the up–down trains are now standing in a long queue."

"Tell the ASM to speak up."

"Hello, Bhalu. AOS Sahib wants to speak to you."

"Yes, Sir!" replied Pawan Kumar in a startled voice.

"Where did the switchman and the porter vanish to?"

"Both of them have left no trace, Sir."

"Your Station Master?"

"Sir. He stays with his family in Rourkela, Sir."

"You go and see for yourself what the matter is."

"But, Sir! Two people have vanished. Sir! This place is a playground of Maoists. Sir, how can I risk my life?"

The young AOS's temper rose.

"You know what the consequence of insubordination is?"

"Yes, Sir! I will go back to my village. I can't do this job. You please send somebody else."

The AOS was perplexed by such a reply. He went to the Sr. DOS's room. Behind him stood the CHC.

A few merchants were sitting in Sr. DOS Rai Sahib's cabin.

"Sir, may I disturb you? An emergency …"

The AOS was panting so much that the CHC had to report the incident instead. "Sir, both, the switchman and the porter, are absconding from Bhalulata station. All the trains are detained, Sir."

"Oh, I see. Maoists had attacked the station a year ago. Am I right?"

"Yes, Sir."

After contemplating for a while, he said, "I am sending the Area Superintendent with a force. Check the mainline—whether it is set, and then, taking the paper line clear from both sides of the station, start the trains with a caution order. I am informing the state government."

Meanwhile, the night was descending. Pawan Kumar did not feel like opening his tiffin box to eat his dinner. Sitting on the chair, he was murmuring to himself, "I am coming, Muniya. I can't carry on like this. I don't mind tending to the buffaloes in the village. Or growing makka-bajra in our fields. But I can't stay here. To hell with this job!"

At Bisra, Mumbai–Howrah Mail kept standing still. The passengers were getting restless. They alighted the train in groups and gheraoed the ASM's cabin with shouts. "Why are you not starting the mail?"

The ASM Bisra was not in a position to pacify the agitating crowd. The Station Master came from his cabin and with folded hands tried to appease the passengers. "Please, calm down. Only for your safety have we detained this train. Maoists have attacked Bhalulata station. They have carried away two of our railway staff; the whole station has come to a halt. How will the train ferry passengers across? You tell us."

The passengers immediately hushed after hearing of the attack. But some still kept arguing, "Why are you keeping us stranded in this place. There is no tea, water or snacks available in this goddamn place. You better take us back to Rourkela station."

Others supported this demand and again started to make noise.

"I shall inform the Control Room. You, people, return back to your compartments." He then passed on the demand to the Control Room.

Meanwhile, the Area Superintendent (ARS) started from Bandhamunda station with his platoon by road. He and the DTI were in one vehicle, while in another van were huddled the RPF Inspector and the armed forces. When they reached Bhalulata station, they entered the closed door of the ASM and took a report from him.

"Is the mainline set?"

"Yes, Sir."

Then he ordered the Control Room, "Move the trains with a caution order. Now I am going to the West cabin."

The DTI requested, "Sir, don't be so impatient. This is a Maoist area. Let dawn break, Sir!"

The ARS was known for his bold and courageous acts. Rejecting the DTI's proposal, he instructed the RPF squad, "Let us go to the West cabin." No motorable road led to the West cabin. Walking slowly on the railway track and ballast, they approached the cabin. The searchlights were scattered all around them. No sound whatsoever escaped the quiet night. The searchlight moved on to the banyan tree which was canopying the West Cabin.

As the searchlights spread and the ARS and his platoon were visible, Govardhan and Tikra moved up the branches to disguise themselves behind the lush leaves.

"This sahib is a monster. Everyone knows about him. The only words that come out of his lips are 'Suspend' and 'Transfer'."

"Shh … Don't move, Tikra. If he sees us, he will butcher us."

Now the ARS climbed into the cabin. Suddenly, from one corner of the cabin flashed two red hot eyes and a ghastly roar. The searchlight dropped from the hands of the ARS. He would have had a nasty fall if the RPF jawans had not been right behind him. He had to be carried down to the Station Master's room in an unconscious state.

The ARS regained his former self when water was sprinkled on his face, but he kept mumbling, "Why are you surrounding me? You bloody fellows go and shoot the bear. I say, shoot it."

The DTI, Jagga Rao, gave a report to the Division Office over the control phone.

"Hello! There is a bear invasion in Bhalulata station and not a Maoist attack!" The news spread fast and thick from the Division Office to the Head Office.

The next day at Chakradharpur's division office, a meeting was called in the early morning to discuss the bear invasion in Bhalulata station. The DRM and all the departmental heads were present. The Sr. DOS announced that ten trains have been affected. Five main express trains have lost their punctuality. The RPF may be instructed to shoot the bear.

The RPF commandant protested. "Sir, we cannot shoot a wild animal. As per the Wildlife Act 1972, it is a punishable offence."

"You please take action. Otherwise, I will call shikaris from Manoharpur station and have them shoot it. I don't know whether my two staff members are dead or have been injured by this bear. I can't wait any longer." The Sr. DOS warned.

"How do you know whether your staff have been injured or killed by this bear? Don't take any hasty decisions. You will have to go to jail afterwards! You inform the Forest Department. They will take proper action."

Cutting through this war of words, the DRM instructed, "Prepare a special train. We will go to the spot, assess the situation and take action accordingly. DFO, Sundergarh may be informed."

Then started Operation Jambaban. With five saloons and one engine, the special train started from Chakradharpur to Bhalulata station. Meanwhile, the DFO did not give permission to shoot the wild animal.

While one night and half a day had passed, the word was spreading about Bhalulata station being invaded by wild bears. The unheard name, Bhalulata, suddenly acquired some fame in the state. Curious passers-by, people of neighbouring villages made a beeline to the site, while one of the cleverer TV channels was quick to dispatch its reporters to capture the never-seen-before footage and soundbites.

The DFO arrived with his subordinates in tow. His refusal to shoot the animal might have been a response to his earlier spat with the Railways. He had been miffed with the Railways for not giving him a free pass to check the illegal ferrying of forest products and costly timber in the trains.

By midday, Bhalulata station had attracted a crowd. Instead of trains, people were found standing on the tracks. On one side of the cabin was the Commandant with his armed RPF platoon; on another side were the DFO and his forest protection forces. The TV channel had made a makeshift podium, on which were seated the crew. Though the Commandant and the DFO were facing each other, they were not on speaking terms. The Commandant was rolling his moustache while the DFO was stroking his beard. Both the groups" body language was bent on showing the other in a poor light.

In front of the cabin were the enthusiastic village folk. They had their indigenous weapons. Some had sickles, some had bhujalis, some had spears, and some came with spikes. Some had sticks and tangias. Whatever they could have laid their hands on, they came with it.

All the noise and commotion outside stirred the bear, which was still trapped inside the cabin. She took a look outside the window and could see a swarm of black heads. A glimpse of the animal from the window sent a ripple through the crowd.

"Why are these RPF and Forest Department people behaving like mute spectators? Why can't they take action?" Murmurs were heard among the restless crowd.

A few minutes ticked by.

Then came a shrieking roar that tore into the land and sky. The astonished crowd was staring at the entrance of the cabin, where the bear was standing—two-legged, like a *Homo erectus*; and in her two hands were two new-born baby cubs. The babies, with their closed eyes, were clasping on to the mother's breast.

The bear, as if inciting the crowd, roared. "Come you civilized, armed people! Catch me, kill me … if you can … if you have the guts … you dare cast evil eyes on my children!"

The spellbound crowd was stunned; they watched a fearless and proud mother with her newborn cubs. Suddenly, their muttering stopped mid-sentence. The birds seemed like they had stopped twittering. The wind seemed like it had ceased whistling.

The RPF's guns came down. The nets, held by the Forest Guards, fell to the ground. The cameras of shutterbugs stopped clicking. The assembled crowd was stunned into a hushed silence, watching a besotted mother, tenderly protecting her innocent new-borns.

The non-threatening silence of the crowd prodded the animal to climb down the stairs with her babies. In the same posture, with two hands full, it trotted to the back of the cabin and slowly disappeared into the jungle.

Now, she is a mother, she is brave; she had no fear, no panic and no fright in her eyes. The vast wilderness of Saranda forest was beckoning to her. The railway personnel, the Forest Armed Forces were breathing a sigh of amazed relief. The assembly of villagers started to melt. Some of them were found muttering, "Why did the bear leave such a vast jungle and come to the station for her delivery? Is it her mother's place?" The public somehow always had the answer. Someone was heard saying, "Don't you know there is no safe haven in the jungle these days for an animal to give birth to their kids. The jungle is on fire. Behind the hills, there is only fire. Fire from the ammunition."

Pomeranian

2UP Mumbai Mail arrived at Bilaspur station on time. It was seven in the morning. During the fifteen-minute stop, the train staff receive a change in duty and the passengers, a good breakfast halt.

Once the train arrived at the platform, it was a replay of the usual scene. The familiar "chai-garam, chai-garam" call of the half-running, half-walking chaiwallah with the clanging of his kettle and his crackling plastic cups as he made the rounds. The creaking fruit cart with overripe bananas and guavas came rolling, mouth-watering dum-aloo poured over sizzling hot pakodas served in sal leaf katoris flew off the hawker boy's basket in minutes; all the while, people got in and got out. Amidst the melee, relatives hovered around doors and monopolized the windows to pamper their dear ones with their endearing ta-ta-bye-byes.

Tearing through the crowd on the platform was a lady rushing towards the brake van. The train was about to leave, and her pace had increased. She could have broken into a sprint but for the high-heeled sandals adorning her feet and a cute Pomeranian in her arms. In between speeding up her pace, she was smothering the doggy with kisses and whispering sweet nothings into his ears.

The lady was middle-aged, attractive and fashionable to boot. Past her forties, she looked well-maintained. Following her quick steps was a uniformed railway staff, otherwise known as the Parcel Babu.

Before blowing the whistle, the train guard was checking the seal of the luggage van and the tailboard of the last bogie, when the running duo reached up to him.

"This dog will go in the dog box," Parcel Babu indicated, breaking through the concentration of the train guard.

"Actually, you see, I had a first-class ticket. My doggy would have travelled with me. But some unkind passengers protested," explained the lady with the doggy.

"True! That Madam had a first-class ticket. But a rule is a rule. These days, people are quoting rules for everything," added the Parcel Babu.

"I have to go today anyway. There is a dog show at Nagpur. There is no other alternative."

"Madam! Please give twenty rupees."

"What? I have already paid for the booking of my doggy. You ask this man." She pointed her finger at the Parcel Babu.

Parcel Babu's gaze was on the platform scene. The green light was already on, signalling for the train to leave the station. Only the whistle of the Guard was left to blow. The ASM started to announce, "Guard and Driver of Mumbai Mail, start your train."

The Guard Babu in a muffled and harried voice said, "Madam, this is not a bribe, it is baksheesh."

"What did you say? Baksheesh? Wait, I will take away your job."

Some more expletives flew through the air. The Guard was not able to hear any more of it.

The dog was reluctant to get into the dog box. He was whimpering and licking the feet of his owner, hoping for some form of relief. Madam gave a kiss to the doggy, caressed his back before handing him over to the Guard, she then returned back to her first-class compartment. To be separated from a loved one can lead to heartache; while walking back to her compartment, our lady was found wiping her eyes with her handkerchief.

"Guard Babu! Please sign the delivery book."

With a whiff of irritation, the Guard signed on the Parcel Babu's delivery book, without even glancing at it and blew the whistle. The wheels started rumbling.

Once in the dog box, the doggy continued to whine.

On the right side of fifty-five, the Guard Babu's long beard was more salt than pepper. The colour of his hair was not visible, concealed as it was by a white cap. The winter overcoat on his white uniform made him look like a Vasco da Gama.

Mulling over the dog owner's comment, the Guard kept blabbering and started rustling through the things in his cabin, the doggy's tin of biscuits, a bundle of newspapers, the railway dak among others.

The doggy, which had been making a sound like a drone, had stopped and now looked as if it had settled down in the dog box. The Guard also let out his stress with a puff and took a deep breath.

"I told your Madam that it is not a bribe. It is a baksheesh. What did she hear? Instead, she started to shout ..."

"Arre, Babu, listen ... where is there no money in play? The peshkar is taking a ghoosh right under the nose of the judge. The Minister, Chief Minister ... they are all taking money! Which is why there is so much brouhaha about corruption? See how many commissions—lokpal ...?"

"When they don't take for themselves, they take for their party."

"You will see—vigilance people, RPF, GRP staff, accounts inspector, commercial inspector—all will come to this cabin. They will check the records. Luggage van, personal cash etcetera; I have to satisfy all of them. Without a handful of baksheesh, how am I to do it?"

The doggy now looked a bit livelier. It perked up its ears, sized up the guard. Perhaps he understood that either he or his Madam was the subject of this outburst.

"Hey, your ears are up! Do you know the consequences of not greasing palms? Then listen. Once what happened ... Konark TV was transporting hundreds of television sets in the luggage van. Before unloading, the coolies asked for a baksheesh of two hundred rupees. The officer of the TV company boasted that his is a government company; no question of bribe, no baksheesh. Later on, half the TV sets were found damaged; the coolies had smashed them on the platform. Who can reform these coolies, tell me?"

"All this bribe-baksheesh in the railways … When will it stop, you know? When there will be three or four railway companies. The guards and conductors of the trains will be like bus conductors, shouting Raipur … Nagpur … Kanpur … Come aboard my train! But this is not going to happen in this lifetime—neither yours nor mine."

The next station arrived. A police inspector came into the cabin. The state police are required to aid with security support to the guard.

Seeing the Inspector, the doggy started to bark. The khaki uniform, the cap and the baton of the Inspector along with his curled moustache made him look like a Veerappan.

"Guard Babu! you seem to be taking a nice companion today."

"Duty, Sir. Duty."

Now the doggy started to bark louder.

"Your police uniform and moustache are what is making him bark."

"No, it is your beard which makes him bark."

Next was Raipur station, the police inspector got down from the luggage van with a loud remark: "One can't sit here."

Then came the accounts and commercial inspectors.

"How is it that today one can see a combination of a cat and a mouse?" commented the guard.

"Inspection of the joint team, you see."

"Hey! Why does the compartment smell foul?" the accounts

inspector was screwing up his nose.

"Can't you see? A doggy is on board. Quite a plump one at that; has worn a nice coat too."

"But why does it smell?" the Commercial Inspector commented, sniffing at the dog box.

The guard, who happened to be an Odia settled in Bilaspur, was suddenly reminded of his school days. He started to hum a poem he had dug out from the memories of his schooldays.

> "Red kohl on the eyes,
>
> Playing in the mango foliage,
>
> Mastering the tunes, plucking the mango buds,
>
> Can the crooning of a crow be that of a cuckoo?
>
> The world will only laugh at the effort."

Then he started translating the Odia poem for the benefit of his non-Odia visitors. "As much as you bathe the doggy with expensive soaps and shampoos, he can never smell as nice as his memsahib."

A roar of laughter reverberated through the cabin. In response, the doggy started barking louder. Perhaps he did not like the derision in their talk—as a customer of the railways, he was not supposed to be the butt of their jokes.

In the next halt, the two visitors got down. The guard then looked into the dog box. Really, the place was stinking. The doggy had urinated, and the liquid had flowed across and wet the bundle of newspapers. Shit! What a mess! He bemoaned and spat out laments. Cleaning all this by himself was a new worry. When there is work to be done, all folks will vanish. Only when there is no work, people will surround him, squat on his trunk and sip tea served by him, along with hot potato chops.

Now he felt like whining and crying. But you need a shoulder to cry on; that enhances the value of crying. But where is the shoulder? Suddenly, he felt he was all alone. Then his thoughts wandered. What is the life of a guard? It is worse than a dog's life. Leaving behind wife and children, one has to roam around like a gypsy, no regularity of eating or sleeping. Whatever fish or mutton one buys for cooking in the Running Room, it tastes so insipid after it has been handled by the railway cook's hand. Sleep in the dormitory is so disturbed, what with all kinds of sounds emanating from the inmates—some snoring, some hollering. The Guard was overwhelmed with self-pity. He could not think further, his mind was so agitated that in protest, he gave a big kick to the dog box. In provocation, the doggy barked even more, got more restless and valiantly moved around inside the box. Then he defecated in protest.

"Hey, I have no time to play with you, you understand. I have to prepare the parcel summary. Then fill up the detention notebook. And so many other sundry tasks are pending for me to attend to."

This set him thinking. *One has to make friends with the doggy; otherwise, the journey will be unbearable.* He remembered the biscuit tin given by the lady. He opened the box and offered one to the doggy. It didn't touch it.

"Hey, are you angry? Or don't you like my face? Of course, I don't have a smooth cheek like your memsahib. In our house, the beard is hereditary, you see. Even my grandfather sported a beard. They all did for some reason, call it disease, detachment. I don't have any such reason. Only thing, my cheeks are rough like that of Om Puri, because of a bout of chickenpox I had during my childhood. To conceal that, I sport a beard. I am a regular domesticated person, you see. I understand your plight. I know how it feels to be separated from your loved ones."

Now he caressed his beard. It was unkempt and dirty, but where would he find the time to groom it?

The train was chugging along, carousing through the jungle, midway between Darekasa and Salekasa. Whenever there was a bend or a crossing, the train zipped along with long whistles. One could see the sky-kissing sal trees, thickets of bamboo passing by on both sides of the moving train.

From the bushes could be heard the mating calls of the peacock, the shrieking of monkeys and some sweet twitters of unnamed birds. The doggy now tore open his belt. His coat slipped off his torso. The Guard saw that he was a male. With his plump and cute look, he had guessed was a bitch.

"Oh, that is why you are so adamant! Didn't like the biscuit with all the shit around, na?" He now felt sorry for the doggy.

"Now, come. Have some fresh air." He then opened the latch of the dog box. "Come and sit here and have your biscuit."

The train was now entering a tunnel. It got pitch dark. The doggy came closer to the Guard, made himself comfortable near his feet and even took a biscuit from him. The Guard Babu then poured some water from his bottle into his mouth. The animosity was turning into friendship.

After the tunnel, came another spot of dense jungle. The trees were even taller and shadier. In between the movement, one could hear the peacock's call and the monkey's shriek.

"Babu re! Don't go near the door. The wheels will run over you. Your tender legs will get cut. Whole life you will become crippled."

Suddenly the train stopped. To know the reason Guard Babu came to the door and holding the handle leaned out to know the reason why the train had stopped.

On the side-lines, not far from the track, a peacock was strutting around with his blue-green feathers. The peahen was picking grains from the ground. From afar, two rabbits were watching the feathered creatures around the bush. Their eyes fell on the fluffy dog. Thinking it to be one of them, they came forward and started running across the rail line. The doggy also thought of them as his clan brothers. Just a long jump from the cabin and he was one of them!

Suddenly, the whistle blew and the train started to move. The Guard came from the door and sat on his seat and looked around.

"Arre ... where is the doggy?"

Next, his eyes fell on the outside, where the doggy was sprinting along with the two rabbits into the jungle.

His head started spinning. He did not know what to do. In a split second, it had escaped. Can he pull the chain and run after the doggy? No, he cannot leave the train. But, what the hell? I am the train guard, he thought. I am the king of the train. I will stay put. You idiot, you go wherever you want to go.

But was it so simple? Thinking about it, he felt stressed. When there will be an enquiry as to what had happened to the dog, which had been under his charge? What would be his reply? He might lose his job. Five people at home were dependent on him. His eldest son is yet to get a job. The daughter is yet to be married off. His anxiety became palpable.

Next halt was Gondia. It is known for its delicious potato chops, fried stuff, and good tea. Passengers got down from their compartments and hovered around the stall and carts, ordering hot savouries. To catch some leftovers and crumbs, an emaciated street dog was hanging around, shaking his legs and salivating.

From the cabin, the Guard Babu's eyes scanned the platform. They fell on the cart. An idea struck him. He got down on to the platform with two biscuits in his hand, went near the dog and tempted him. "Chuchu … chuchu … chuchu …"

The smell of the biscuits was too much for the hungry bedraggled street dog. His entire life he had survived on food wasted by the passengers. Forget about the taste, he had never even smelt something so delicious. Attracted by the bait, he came behind the Guard and jumped into the cabin. Seizing the moment, Guard Babu pounced on him with the velvet coat of the "phoren" doggy and tied the belt on him. Then he pushed him into the dog box and latched him there.

There was not a hint of the slightest protest from the street dog. Fed with delicious biscuits and with warm clothes on, he fell into a nice snooze.

The Guard Babu was smiling, thinking about how there are people who are peaceful and happy even in captivity. No wonder some people like to remain even in jail. He was reminded of a person called Natia from his village who used to steal coconuts and small items, who would frequently land up in jail only to get free meals.

Nagpur arrived. The Guard Babu had packed his luggage well

before and was well-prepared. The halt was for half an hour, as the engines would have to be changed along with a change of duty for the guard. Handing over the parcels, along with the dog box to his reliever, the Guard Babu quickly got down from the train and started walking behind the box boy, towards the Running Room, humming a tune, a whistle on his lips.

A group of friends and well-wishers had gathered to welcome our fashionable lady in the first-class compartment. It may have been that the welcome greetings of her friends delayed her arrival to the guard's cabin.

Negotiating between the carts full of oranges, bananas, guavas on the platform, the Guard Babu kept briskly walking towards the Running Room while visualizing the scene when the lady would discover the contents in the dog box—a scruffy, dishevelled, emaciated street dog instead of her white-as-milk, fluffy, cute Pomeranian. She might shout and scream, "Oh my God! Where is my Bunty? Whose dog is this? Where is the bearded guard? Wait and watch … I am going to take away his job."

But how could she? No details of the dog had been mentioned in the waybill—not the colour, the type, or the breed of the dog that had been left in the charge of the guard. Who will catch him?

Sleeping Pill

An AC first-class coach of the Delhi–Howrah–Rajdhani Express, on a certain night, saw three foreigners and one Indian travelling together.

The first to enter the compartment was the Indian passenger. Dark, bearded, medium-built, and middle-aged, he entered the compartment panting, sweating with his suitcases, airbags, a clutch bag *et al*—all in a huff to establish the ownership of his berth. A total of five pieces of luggage were brought in by his coolie and were all fitted snugly under the berth. The usual haggling and paying the coolie was over. Now, our passenger smiled, proud of himself; he switched on the fan and spread himself out on the lower berth.

The second passenger was a Chinese gentleman. Slim, fair, and young, he appeared to be a tourist. No doubt, his luggage was on the lighter side. On his waistband was his cell phone and necessary items. He entered the compartment demurely, greeted the Indian with a bow, and took to his berth.

The third passenger was South African. Tall, black, muscular with curly hair, he appeared middle-aged, probably in his forties. Pushing his luggage and talking on his cell phone simultaneously, he entered the compartment, his all-consuming laughter shaking him to the bone. He appeared to be among the international-seminar-trotting types.

The passenger who entered the compartment last was an American. He entered only five minutes before the train was to leave. Strong and stout like a Holstein bull, he had a heavy piece of luggage strapped to his back. His head didn't boast much hair, but whatever little there was fluttered under the fan. He had seen on the reservation chart that he had been allotted an upper berth. In his natural effusive manner, he greeted everyone with a "hello, everybody" and declared, "I will take the lower berth."

The lower berth had been allotted to the Chinese passenger. On hearing the bulky American, he got up from his berth with alacrity and transferred his bag to the upper one, feeling it wiser to shift. Perhaps he felt that sleeping under the big hulk of such a person could invite some trouble. Soft-spoken with gentle eyes, it was difficult to fathom what was going on his mind. Like a good boy, he clambered to the upper berth.

In the meantime, the AC attendant had put a bouquet of roses in the holder of the panel of the compartment. Neatly arranged linen, blankets, and bedsheets were kept aside. The bearer of the pantry car served the guests welcome drinks and chocolates.

The introductory session among the passengers ended thanks to the garrulous American who took the lead. It transpired that he was the Vice President of an IT company in the States and was touring India on a business trip. The Chinese passenger was a tourist in the real sense. He was conducting research on the Buddhist Viharas in India. The African was a doctor; he had come to attend an international seminar on AIDS. The Indian was a professor. After having given a talk in Delhi University, he was on his way to Vishwa Bharati to deliver another.

The train was already in motion, and soon it picked up full speed. Half an hour later, the bearer came, arranged the centre table, and kept trays of snacks on it: a spread of hot samosas, roasted kaju, mixed savouries, and assorted sweets. Seeing this, the American, his gaze fixed on the Indian, commented, "Here people indulge you with a lot of food. Indians are quite hospitable, I must say."

The gentleman from India smilingly nodded in agreement and thought to himself that this was absolutely true. Once he had gone to the USA for a meeting, where not even a cup of tea or coffee had been served the entire day; rather, it had been announced that the participants could help themselves to beverages from the vending machines by paying for it themselves. If that meeting had been held in India, the clatter of teacups and saucers, along with snacks and cutlery, would have been heard for the most part of the day.

After the high tea was over, the bearer took their orders for dinner. The three foreigners ordered continental food, while the Indian ordered a vegetarian Indian meal. At about 8 in the evening, soup was served. Then came the continental dishes for the three foreigners. For the Indian passenger came two pieces of roti, some dal, and vegetables.

Before the setting of their dinner, the American had opened his bottle of whisky. On his instructions, the attendant came with wine glasses. The American poured the drinks into the decanters and offered them to his co-passengers. The Chinese hesitated a bit and then coyly accepted his offering. The African merrily grabbed the glass. The Indian said, "No thanks, I am a teetotaller."

Seeing the Spartan food habits of the Indian, the American exclaimed, "Hey! You are really great. Simple living and high thinking, I must say. You are a holy man. Can I call you Swamiji? Will you mind?"

The Indian simply nodded and smiled.

Soon the American's plate was wiped clean. He called the waiter for more food. More chicken and salad were served. It was evident that he was doing justice to his great bulk.

The African also tucked into his plate. After it was finished, he took out one cigar from his suitcase and lit it. Without anybody asking, he commented, "Without one of these, I will not get any sleep."

Smoking and drinking are prohibited in the railway compartments. But none of the railway employees was objecting to it; they were cooperating by looking the other way when the guests were indulging their cravings. Hospitable country indeed!

The Indian was also thinking along the same lines. *How hospitable we are!* The smoke from one side of the coach and the smell of the liquor from the other was too much for him; nonetheless, he was putting up with it good-naturedly.

The clock struck ten. The American was not yet done with his food and drinks. The African's cigar was like sugarcane and showed no signs of waning. Due to the smoke or whatever else, the Chinese man started to cough and went to the washroom with his small bag.

Finally, the food plates, the trays, the spoons, the forks were all taken away, but the glass in the American's hand was not emptying. To sleep soundly, he admitted loudly for the benefit of his co-passengers, he needed two more pegs.

The Chinese came back from the washroom and climbed to the upper berth. Once on the berth, he started shaking his arms and legs vigorously like a dying lizard. The bearer, who had come to clean the centre table, noticed this and asked, "Sir, shall I call the train superintendent?"

The African commented, "You don't need to worry. This is his usual preparation for going to sleep. He has taken drugs."

The Indian lying on the lower berth was trying to catch some sleep, when the African's comment made him blurt out to himself, "Great is the all-tolerant Indian Railways. Drunkards, drug addicts, fraudsters, thieves, vagabonds … all are being carried in the lap of the great railways. No anger, no hatred, no opposition, no animosity, no enmity, no eyebrows raised, no nose turned up."

His thoughts were interrupted by the American, who asked in a patronizing tone, "Swamiji, don't you need any sleeping pills?"

Swamiji gave him a mysterious smile. He sat up from his horizontal position and pulled out a suitcase from under the berth. Then he gave a small nudge to the box, opened it, and said, "Get up, my *son*. Come kiss me. I am not getting any sleep."

His son was deep in sleep. The Indian then slapped his back. The son raised his head with a hiss, shook itself, and hit the quivering down-turned palms of the Swamiji twice. Then kissing the shrinking hood of the pet, the Indian put him inside the box and said, "Now, go to sleep my son."

The American turned to stone, the wine glass frozen in his hand. The cigar fell from the African's mouth. The trembling body of the Chinese man on the upper berth became still.

Within no time, the three travellers, one by one, hopped out of the first-class coach like frogs.

The Serpent

The story begins in a first-class compartment of the Howrah–Ahmedabad Express, in the late hours of a rainy night. It unfolds along with the movement of the train, which goes up the hills and down the valleys. The train halts at the stations, but the story doesn't cease. How can such a story about humans ever come to an end? It knows no breaks, no interlude, no pause, no intermission. Has there ever been a finishing line to the ever-flowing march of human history?

The hero of our story is a railway officer. A young direct recruit, about twenty-five, bubbling with dreams and passions—but a greenhorn to the railways. Like all young men, his eyes sparkled with hopes and dreams of a rosy future, his persona oozed with such sincerity and dollops of self-confidence that it seemed as if all the trains, with his magical touch, could reach their destination before time. With such vibrant and lively characters around, the serving railway employees of the division could be inspired and become epitomes of courtesy and selfless service.

After completing the foundation course at Mussoorie, our hero joined the South Eastern Railways. Two years of probation, within which he was supposed to do a Bharat Darshan tour, which included visits to railway stations, parcel offices, goods sheds, reservation offices, coal mines, steel factories … all as part of the training. Before going on this Bharat Darshan, our hero was on his way to the Railway Staff College, Baroda, to acquaint himself with preliminary knowledge about the Indian Railways.

The train arrived at Chakradharpur (CKP) station at 1.30

a.m. in the night. The change of guard took place at this station. Conductors of Kharagpur divisionhanded over the charge to their counterparts at Chakradharpur. The new conductor, after being introduced to our hero, allotted him a lower berth in the first-class compartment. On getting the berth, our hero settled into his seat, with his bag and baggage in place. After this, what else was left for him to do other than sleep? He could scarce read a book, as it might have disturbed the other passengers. Besides, there was no way of getting to know any of his other co-travellers—all of them covered, from head to foot, in that damp rainy night. Hence, sleeping was the only natural thing to do.

But our hero would not get a wink of sleep as his young was head crowded with all sorts of domestic thoughts: *must construct a house in his village, help the younger brother complete his studies in college, and find a suitable groom for the younger sister*. Only some of the items on his list of unfinished tasks. But then, our hero was not sanguine if other tasks werenot to crop up after all these responsibilities ended. So it was better to banish all worries and let sleep take over. This was what he told himself.

The morning after, our hero was taking a while to rise from his sleep. It was a lazy morning. But what was this? As soon as he opened his eyes, his big yawn stopped midway and his posture changed— from horizontal to lotus!

What could be the reason? Not far to seek an answer. The adjacent lower berth was occupied by a woman, and a young one to boot. She could not be more than twenty, guessed our hero, though he always found it difficult to guess the right age of women.

We can call the young lady the heroine of our story. Though not devastatingly beautiful, she definitely had plenty of oomph and charm, which made one's eyes remain gazing upon her face for a long time. Fair of skin, with a sharp and dainty nose, doe-shaped lively eyes, she was endowed with black, lustrous hair, though it was cut short in tune with the times. Her appearance suggested that she was of a Bengali origin, and our hero wondered which film actress she could be compared with—Moon Moon Sen? Aparna Sen? No ... no ... well, even if not in the likeness of the regal Suchitra Sen, she could pass off as more beautiful than the other two.

Now, who can define beauty? Is there any yardstick for female beauty? Well, our hero was reminded of the Bard's saying: "Beauty lies in the eyes of the beholder." Has beauty something to do with age? The first flush of youth had caressed our heroine with the bounty of spring and drenched her with the beauty and fragrance of fresh roses. Even apes look beautiful with the onset of youth, so say the Sanskrit poets. Our hero was also of the same age, where one's mind was always humming amorous tunes, amidst all the noise. And for a young man, what could be more overwhelming than the sight of a pretty young woman for company?

The same can be said of the opposite side too. The proximity of a handsome youth can be slightly unsettling for any young woman.

"Good Morning. Where are you travelling to?"

"Baroda. What about you?"

"Ahmedabad. You boarded around midnight from some station, na?"

"Ya. You? Perhaps from Kolkata?"

"Ya. How did you know?"

"Just guessing."

"Sir! Tea," the bearer saluted.

The train had arrived at Jharsuguda. After Kolkata, if one wanted the best tea or coffee, it was to be found at this station. Since the train did not have a pantry car, a message had been conveyed to Jharsuguda station.

"Bearer! One more flask of tea for memsahib. Quick!"

"Do you work with the railways?"

"How did you know?"

"Again, just guessing."

Both of them broke into laughter.

"Do take some biscuits with the tea. It won't lead to acidity." Our heroine extended a packet of biscuits.

"Are you a doctor?" Our hero was curious.

"Ya, I'm studying medicine. How did you know?"

"Haha, just guessing."

"So, our guesses are spot on."

Again they broke into another round of synchronous laughter. Amidst this pleasant banter, a third character got up from his slumber, rubbing his eyes. In the meantime, another flask of tea had arrived. The train left the station.

"Get up, Khokan, have tea!"

Our hero looked towards the upper berth.

"Oh! Is he your younger brother?"

"Ya."

While sipping their morning cuppa, some more facts about each other were collected and verified. Our hero, as we already know, was a probationary officer with the railways, on his way for training to Baroda. Our heroine revealed that she too came from a railway family. Her father was an engineer in the railways, so she was accustomed to its style and ways. She was studying medicine in Moscow. She was visiting a relative in Ahmedabad.

Now, the younger brother of the heroine can be called the fool of the pack. He was much younger than our heroine, perhaps ten or twelve years of difference between them. Round cherubic face, chubby cheeks with his body plump ... the cuddly younger brother could evoke amused affection in anybody. However, more than eliciting amusement, our hero felt smug; there would be no threat from the younger brother. He could spend hours talking to the girl without any fear of disapproval.

In such situations, the very young sibling, instead of being a roadblock, can help the process; from fertilization to germination to further advancements in an incipient relationship. So our hero felt assured that he could row the boat of sweet romantic talk with the heroine, unopposed and uninterrupted. Further, to add flavour to the budding romance, the fourth berth in the compartment lay empty.

How could that be the case? Normally, Ahmedabad Express was the only direct train for the expat Gujaratis in Kolkata. It always ran a crowd. Tickets were booked two months in advance. How did such a situation come to pass on that day?

The situation was such that though it was the only direct train from Kolkata to Ahmedabad, there was nothing to boast about regarding this train. If there had been a prize for a decrepit train, this one would have won, hands-down. To make matters worse, the pouring rains of the previous night had created some sort of leak in the upper berth of the compartment, due to which the conductor had shifted the passenger to another bogie.

When the extended tea-time came to an end, the younger brother rushed to the washroom to attend nature's call, a towel in hand. But how was it that our hero was not feeling any such pressure? He had not shown any urgency to head to the washroom. Was that morning such a golden and entirely novel experience for our hero? Was there no room for him to attend to the daily and dirty routines, and just because the chit-chat kept becoming sweeter and more enjoyable with the passing of each moment?

Our hero was on an upward swing; he was singing to himself, talking to himself. What a beautiful match they would make; by the time he finished his probationary period, she would have completed her medicine course. The daughter of a railway engineer, so beautiful and accomplished! Their match would surely be a big hit in social circles. So she would be his memsahib. When our heroine rose from the berth to take her vanity purse off from the hook on the side of the coach, our hero also stood up and cleverly measured her height against his. It was just the right stature.

Meanwhile, ample cups of tea had been consumed, and it had done its work on our hero. He could no longer put it off. Nature's call had to be heeded, and its urgency made our hero finally get up from his seat. He rushed to the toilet only to come out of it chuckling.

"What happened? Why so much mirth?"

"Your brother … Khokan …"

When our hero got excited, his words would get warbled, and he would swallow them up.

"What happened? Tell me frankly, na."

"The bathroom is open and Khokan is fully …"

"Oh!" Our heroine also joined in on the laughter. Her sparkling giggle washed away whatever formality stood between them. "This must be the doing of your railway's doors," our clever heroine commented and went to inspect her brother in his situation.

Thereafter, there was no counting of hours. The rains had given way to bright sunshine, and the territory of Odisha had given way to the terrain of Madhya Pradesh and beyond. None kept track of when breakfast was over and when lunch had been served and eaten; the happy banter was only broken intermittently by hawkers: pakorawallah, kelawallah, badamwallah, chaiwallah. Most of them were patronized by the fool played by the brother. In between relishing and digesting the eatables, his queries—"Which river is this?", "Which dam is this?"—were the only irritants for our hero. He wished that the junior would consume all the food and go on a six-month-long slumber like Kumbhkarna.

That day, the whole world looked colourful. The entire universe seemed to overflow with joy and ecstasy. The distant horizon was covered with the cool canopy of the blue sky. Mother earth was almost as if offering its green trophy as an homage to the gods of the sky. The naughty wind was flirting and caressing the paddy stalks on the fields. The verdant carpets on both sides of the rail track were greener than ever and the intervening jungles more delightful. The distant hills were looking splendorous in their height, and the blue sky was dotted with flocks of birds; their twitter was like a symphony conducted in the air. Everywhere, there was a celebration of life and of its youthful exuberance.

Our hero was imagining that he was not travelling in a ramshackle train of the Indian Railways but was mounted on a shining white, flying stallion, which was flying them beyond the clouds, the moon and the stars, to an unknown fairyland.

In the meantime, another big station had come—Nagpur. They bought oranges, bhusavali bananas and seedless grapes. More expenses were incurred all throughout the journey, happily, by our hero. Smitten by our enchantress heroine, our hero's demeanour was suave, his smiles hearty and conversation polished; in fact, all the arsenals of sophistications were in full display, all through the journey.

After dinner, our heroine was naturally feeling sleepy, while sleep had escaped our hero's eyes. He was imagining what it would be like if the train journey could have been endless, despite the leaking roof, the dirty compartment, the rattling motion of the train. He wished his destination would never arrive. Like a satellite, the train would revolve round a planet, day and night, month after month, year after year. This golden trip would then become immortal. The happy hours spent on this memorable day would remain eternal.

In the course of the conversation, our hero had skilfully highlighted all the positive aspects about himself: his status as a Class I officer, his hobbies like reading, writing, and sports. When it came to his family and background, it was mostly an exaggeration and less a fact. More water than milk. How could he reveal that he was born in an unheard-of village, in a backward area? Where a motorcycle makes the urchins run after it for a mile, to whose land the rain god is so unkind that nothing grows, where cows do not give milk as much as manure, where the thatched roofs are so low that one has to bend to avoid their prickling. Would he say that he belongs to Delhi instead of Odisha?

Our hero knew telling the truth courageously happened only in Bollywood films, where the protagonists on the celluloid screen swear everlasting love even if they come from radically different backgrounds. The heroine would have taken the first plunge into the ocean of love knowing well the modest background of the hero.

But where is the place for such emotional intensity in the real world? The contrast between the dream world and the real world was glaring, like that between heaven and hell. Even the birds go back to the shade of the trees when they face the hot sun, he surmised.

"No, but I will not take such a self-defeating step. I will create my own reality." This was our hero's new-age musings that he presumed would make his dream a reality.

But what the heck? What is happening? Where is the story drifting, with only two characters, the hero and the heroine? Is there no other character in this story, one who can bring about some momentum and take the story forward to its happy ending? Does our hero need a villain to do the impossible, to win over his lady love? The readers must be eagerly awaiting the appearance of a villain who alone can cement the wide chasm between the two.

Well, there indeed was a villain in the tale. Not the usual ones—with bloodshot eyes, a shaven head and the flex of rippling muscles—a la the filmy ones! He would come onstage only at the appropriate time. The villain of our story is extremely dangerous. But he is scared of daylight. He is someone who is powerless before the Sun God. The darkness of the night is his friend. The quiet of the night is his ally. So he would come, tiptoeing in the deathly hours of the night.

The villain of our story is a serpent. Well, that should not come as a surprise. Was not the serpent the first villain of civilization? The devil came to Paradise in the guise of a serpent. The first creation of the Creator, Adam and Eve, how happily they lived and how blissfully they had been cavorting around under the protective care of the Almighty, until Satan could not tolerate this happiness anymore and tempted the couple to bite the forbidden fruit.

The night was getting darker and deeper. Rains of the previous night had returned with a vengeance. The dilapidated roof of the train was taking the hit. The torrential rain beat upon it with sounds that resembled the pelting of pebbles. The whistling sound of the wind was reverberating through the compartment and the rain lashing all around them.

The serpent, which had slipped into the compartment earlier, was growing virulent. Rains make the serpent more potent, while all the other animals, like birds and insects, grow number under the spell; a sort of languor grips them. Animals and birds, cuddling their offspring, go into a deep slumber in their nesting holes, crevices, and all possible niches. Only the serpent gets out of his cavern. Neither scared of the torrential rains, nor of the sludge and muck around, it is the only creature who comes out to prey on the hapless rain-terrified creatures.

The night was getting older, and with it grew the ferocity of the serpent. An unknown thrill was gripping it. Our hero was completely under its spell. He felt like something was desperately trying to escape his being. A star, which was as if trying to defect to a different orbit.

What a lovely day it had been, what tingling happiness and exhilaration throughout. But what is this? All those heavenly feelings were now getting crushed under the weight of the serpent. What does a villain do? The villain's work is to go on a rampage and to trample on the beautiful treasure troves.

In the adjacent berth, our heroine was blissfully asleep. A lovely dream was replaying on her dreamy eyelids. In that dim-blue light of the compartment, her two feet, from under the sheet were like the lissom petals of a white lotus. The deadly serpent, in full form, wanted to recoil on the white lotus as it would have in a pond, full of such supple lotus stalks. When she turned, it looked like a lovely flower bush, which the deadly serpent wanted to sneak into and crush.

The rain was relentless. As if someone in the sky was emptying out pots and pots of water on the earth. The serpent was getting restless. It was now trying to spread its hood and was ready to attack. Its quivering, red, flared-up tongue looked ominous.

Our terrified hero was frightened to death. He was shivering. Will there be a catastrophe? He was desperately trying to get out of the clutch of the serpent and was perspiring heavily. Somehow, he managed to get up and open the windows.

A gust of wind came in, and with it, the shirt hanging on the hook fell down along with some papers. When our hero tried to switch on the light, something else fell. Was it an owl that had jumped into the semi-darkness of the compartment? Was it some bad omen?

Our hero picked up the purse that had slipped out of his shirt pocket, and with it some papers and a photo. In that faint blue light, our hero picked up the photo and looked at it. Another round of perspiration bathed him.

Slowly, a few scenes flashed before his eyes. The engagement ceremony in the temple, along with the parents from both sides, the bashful face of the girl surrounded by her friends, her furtive glances at him, the feast, the acceptance from both sides and the sweet anticipation of a rosy future.

But here, in this compartment, in that rain-soaked night, our hero was gradually becoming besotted with his new find. His love was not able to fathom these obstacles.

Another voice rings in: "What is love? Do you know what it means? Is it a passion, a weakness, an infatuation or an accident? Is libido the definition of love? Is love not a sacrifice? A silent surrender?"

From the other side, the hissing sound of the serpent went on unabated.

A voice whispered: "The photowali is your parents' choice. Only the engagement has been done; nothing more than that. You could return the advanced gift of money. The train companion is educated, accomplished, beautiful, and city-bred. She can accompany you to clubs, hotels, and social gatherings. She would be a perfect match for your professional standing and status. Listen to this voice! Don't leave a lifetime chance of plucking such lovely low-lying fruit."

Our hero was bewildered by the many voices from all sides. One voice said that he would be consumed by this spark, which would become a blazing fire. The other voice said that this was the moment, and he should seize it for a fun-filled life.

Our hero was sliced by a double-edged knife. What would he do?

The morning after, our hero discovered that the serpent had bitten itself. It was lying listless, poisoned by its own venom. His hood and body were broken to pieces.

But there is no death for the serpent. Till the sun and stars move the universe, till life goes on in the earth, the serpent will remain alive and kicking. But on that day, it was lying, vanquished.

In the berth in front of him, our heroine was sleeping like a calm and composed goddess. A slight and benign smile quivered on her lips. Had the serpent not failed to overpower her, such a beatific precious smile would not have been playing on her lips. If the serpent had been victorious, there would have been no fragrance in the flowers. There would be no nectar, only a surfeit of venom. The betrothed girl would not have an assured smile, but a life that had been rejected and full of pathos.

If the serpent had won, life, as in Hobbes's word, would have been, "nasty, brutish, and short".

The dew of the night was melting away under the morning sun, like qualms melting away from our hero's mind. Getting down at Baroda station, carrying his handbag, suitcase, and all his assorted work-related manuals, our hero walked away, slowly into the crowd, with his head bent under the weight of guilt. He realized that it was he who had morphed into a deadly serpent the previous night.

Acknowledgements

At the outset, I express my sincere thanks to Ms Malabika Patel, who graciously took the pains of translating my stories from original Odia to English, thereby giving me a pan-India recognition.

While doing research for the novel, I drew upon the facts contained in the books *An Engineering Feat-Construction of Koraput-Rayagada New Railway Line* by Shri A. Bhima Rao, the then-Chief Administrative Officer of South Eastern Railway; *Building the Railway of the Raj (1850–1909)* by Ian J. Kerr; and the *South Eastern Railway-March to New Millennium* by Shri R.R. Bhandari. I am thankful to all of them.

More than three decades of railway service, in addition to providing me with my daily bread, gave me tremendous insights, which prompted me to write stories based on my railway experience. I am beholden to the Indian Railways. I came across many staff members, high and not-so-high, who were very loyal to the Indian Railways and who showered love and affection on me. My stories are a tribute to such people. Many of my stories are modelled on the selfless characters of my subordinate staff.

My erstwhile bosses and senior colleagues who though not directly connected with publication of the book, but to whom I am indebted for instilling fellow feeling and empathy during the rough and tumble of my railway service are Late Shri R.C. Saxena, Shri Jeetendra Kumar, Shri T. Kumardas, Shri B. Rangarajan, Shri R.C. Das, Shri Bhaskar Chaudhury, Shri Pramod Kumar, Shri Asit Gupta, Shri L.N. Sadangi, Shri M. S. Jayant and Shri H.S. Joshi.

My sincere thanks to Ms Ateendriya Dasgupta of Leadstart Publishing Private Ltd for her invaluable editorial inputs.

Last but not the least, I am hugely indebted to Leadstart Publishing Private Ltd, but for whom, this book would not have been in your hands. By taking up publication of this book, my second one, after *Rail Romance*, they have reposed their faith in me as a writer. I owe it all to them.

About the Translator

A banker by profession, Malabika Patel retired from the Reserve Bank of India as General Manager in 2016 and is presently settled in Bhubaneswar. Literature, both Odia and English, fascinates Malabika. She loves translating rare old Odia documents and classics into English.

Malabika Patel

Contact No: 9920375401

Email id: patelmalabika@gmail.com

Glossary

ARS - Area Superintendent

AOS - Assistant Operating Superintendent

ASM - Assistant Station Master

CCM - Chief Commercial Manager

CE - Chief Engineer

CE (Con) - Chief Engineer (Construction)

CHC - Chief Controller

CME - Chief Mechanical Engineer

COM - Chief Operations Manager

CPO - Chief Personnel Officer

CPRO - Chief Public Relations Officer

CSTE - Chief Signal & Telecom Engineer

DEN - Divisional Engineer

DME (P) - Divisional Mechanical Engineer (Power)

DPO - Divisional Personnel Officer

DRM - Divisional Railway Manager

DRUCC - Divisional Railway Users Consultative Committee

DS - Divisional Superintendent

DTI - Divisional Traffic Inspector

Dy CHC - Deputy Chief Controller

Dy CPO (Gaz) - Deputy Chief Personnel Officer (Gazetted)

Dy CE (Con) - Deputy Chief Engineer (Construction)

FA&CAO - Financial Advisor & Chief Accounts Officer

GM - General Manager

GRP - Government Railway Police

IG (RPF) - Inspector General (Railway Protection Force)

IOW - Inspector of Works

KK Line - Kottavalasa Kirandul Line

KR Line - Koraput Rayagada Line

PWI - Permanent Way Inspector

RITES - Rail India Technical & Economic Services

Sr. DOS - Senior Divisional Operating Superintendent

Sr. DOM - Senior Divisional Operations Manager

Sr. DCM - Senior Divisional Commercial Manager

Sr. DME - Senior Divisional Mechanical Engineer

Sr. DME (C&W) - Senior Divisional Mechanical Engineer (Carriage & Wagon)

Sr. DSTE - Senior Divisional Signal &Telecom Engineer

Sr. DEE (OP) - Senior Divisional Electrical Engineer (Operations)

ZRUCC - Zonal Railway Users Consultative Committee